Kathleen Bartholomew

KATHLEEN BARTHOLOMEW

NELL GWYNNE'S
ON LAND
AND AT SEA

NELL GWYNNE'S

ON LAND

AND AT SEA

or,

WHO WE DID ON
OUR SUMMER HOLIDAYS

Kage Baker
Kathleen Bartholomew

Illustrated by J. K. Potter

SUBTERRANEAN PRESS 2012

First Edition

ISBN
978-1-59606-464-5

Subterranean Press
PO Box 190106
Burton, MI 48519

www.subterraneanpress.com

Dedication:

This one is finally for Kage herself. We finished it, kiddo.
Et ceciderunt prosequitur percussive

I N THE YEAR 1848 there was, in the vicinity of Whitehall, an exclusive dining establishment catering to many of those distinguished gentlemen who might be observed going in and out of the Houses of Parliament. Its customers were by no means limited to statesmen and peers, however; Royal Society members, journalists, and other prominent and powerful personages dined there as well.

Several floors beneath the restaurant, communicating with it by means of a cleverly-concealed ascending room, was an even more exclusive establishment with a somewhat more limited clientele. Its membership was by invitation only, and invitations were generally extended only to persons likely to be privy to official secrets. The place was called Nell Gwynne's, and was, to be perfectly plain, a brothel.

However...

Do not imagine, Reader, that Nell Gwynne's was in any way a conventional house of ill repute. Its staff were, one and

all, gentlewomen of some education who possessed certain talents (beyond those skills with which a reasonably experienced whore might be supposed to be familiar) that might have astonished their regular clientele, had they ever had occasion to learn of them. The artful extraction and retail of official secrets was foremost, but now and then the judicious use of firearms, code decryption or explosives might be required.

ON THE THIRTIETH of June a rare mood prevailed in the elegantly-appointed chambers far below King Street. There was a wistfulness amongst the gentlemen customers being entertained, and a certain blitheness amongst the ladies doing the entertaining, and for the same reason: Nell Gwynne's was about to undergo its annual closure for its summer holidays. For the space of an entire month, Nell Gwynne's regular customers would be obliged to seek their fornication elsewhere, as its staff would spend four weeks at the seaside.

The business of a brothel is at bottom a banal one. The solaces of the flesh are the common privilege of every man, upstairs or down, and so the habitués of Nell Gwynne's paid more for characterization, theatrical detail and a certain specificity of satiation than for the simple act of sexual congress. They also expected a higher level of attention from their demi-mondaines, and thus the more sensitive patrons were aware that underlying the ladies' enthusiasm (which could not honestly be denied) was their happy anticipation of well-earned holidays.

Mrs. Otley, who wore a jockey's silks and employed, amongst other things, a bit and bridle, plied her riding crop today with a shade more cheery liberality than was her custom on the buttocks of Sir Arthur H., who whinnied appreciatively as he bore her around the room. Across the hall Miss Rendlesham, who presided over a chamber got up as a schoolroom, was belaboring likewise the buttocks of Lord Q., bent over a form and roaring as he promised to be a good boy henceforth. Privately, however, he felt that she wielded her birch rod with something less than her customary sternness.

In the next room over, Herbertina Lovelace, who affected midshipman's garb and wore her hair cropped, counterfeited tearful protests as she dropped her trousers for Sir Dennis F. Sir Dennis was gaudily dressed in a naval costume to which he was not, in fact, entitled, never having got any nearer to armed service than strolling near the Horse Guards' parade ground. It was just as well Herbertina presented her back to Sir Dennis, for otherwise he might have detected a certain insincere sparkle in her eyes as she begged the great fierce admiral not to shockingly abuse a poor young man so.

Major-General Francis P., on the other hand, while more than entitled to his uniform and a chestful of medals beside, had elected to wear a golden wig and schoolgirl's frock today as he simulated sapphic delights with the three Devere sisters, Jane, Dora and Maude. If their squeals of merriment were a bit more gleeful than was customary, the Major-General didn't mind; *he* liked jolliness in his little friends.

Even Lady Beatrice (a pseudonym, employed out of respect for her late father's name), who was customarily of a work-womanlike disposition, might have been seen to exhibit a certain absent-mindedness in her attention to her duties. However, as she was presently clad solely in a layer of pale powder and a black velvet collar, and was, besides, impersonating a recently deceased person at the request of the Honorable Edwin J., she was not taxed in her contemplation of a month's sunny leisure while that gentleman wept over her corpse and frenziedly abused himself. And, fortunately, the Honorable Edwin J. was not an exceptionally observant youth.

One by one, as their lusts were seen to, the respective gentlemen were dressed and ushered on their way to the ascending room, whence they departed after a final cigar or glass of brandy (or, for the Honorable Edwin J., lemon squash) in the reception parlor.

"Hurrah!" cried Herbertina, shrugging out of her brass-buttoned jacket. "Here's to blessed chastity!"

"Here's to the whole month of July!" Jane danced a few steps of a Highland Fling.

"Here's to the balmy breezes of Torbay!" Dora pretended to snap castanets with her fingers. Lady Beatrice emerged from her changing room at this point, still powdered a ghostly white, and sprinted ahead of the others.

"First to the baths!" she called gaily, and the others raced after her, shedding garments as they went.

At the other end of the corridor, a somewhat less convivial scene was taking place. Mrs. Corvey, the proprietress of Nell Gwynne's, sat in her office regarding Mrs. Merridge, the establishment's cook. Mrs. Merridge avoided Mrs. Corvey's eyes, not out of any particular sense of guilt but because Mrs. Corvey had none.

Which is to say, Mrs. Corvey did not possess human eyes. Having lost her sight as a consequence of working in a pin factory by limited light for most of her childhood, she had readily agreed when the artificers of the Gentleman's

Speculative Society (which discreet organization underwrote Nell Gwynne's) invited her to undergo an experimental process intended to restore vision. Her black goggles concealed a pair of optical implants which, although providing her with superior sight by day, by night and by infrared as well as having a telescopic function, did not in any manner resemble *eyes*.

"This is rather short notice, Mrs. Merridge," said Mrs. Corvey.

"I can't help that, Ma'am," Mrs. Merridge replied. "It come on me sudden. My brother gave me this tract what opened my eyes to sinfulness. I asked myself, what would Jesus say if I was to meet Him right now? And I can't think He'd approve of the way I earn my wages, you know."

"But you aren't a whore, Mrs. Merridge," said Mrs. Corvey. "You simply cook for them. It says in the Bible our Lord dined with sinners and publicans, don't it? Now, who do you suppose done the cooking for them? Somebody had to."

"Yes. Well. Be that as it may," said Mrs. Merridge. "What do you expect our Lord would have to say to *you*, eh?"

"To *me*? 'Sorry about the eyes, dear, just do the best you can'?" Mrs. Corvey guessed acidly. "Right, then, Mrs. Merridge, if you must go, you must. The Gentlemen will have something to say about it, however."

Mrs. Merridge went a little pale. "I'm not telling none of your secrets! I signed that paper, didn't I?"

The Gentlemen in question were those of the Speculative Society, of course. Operating out of a subterranean lair under Craig's Court connected to Nell Gwynne's by hidden tunnels, they were the recipients of all intelligence gathered therein, and had provided Mrs. Corvey not only with her new eyes but a number of other useful devices. Unfortunately, dependable servants were not among these devices, and Mrs. Corvey had to deal with the age-old vagaries of cooks as personally as any other London lady.

"To be sure, you did, Mrs. Merridge," said Mrs. Corvey, with a sniff. "They'll want to debrief you, all the same."

Wondering uneasily what *debrief* might mean, Mrs. Merridge said, "I'm sure I've always been a woman of my word!"

"No doubt. It's out of my hands now, I fear," said Mrs. Corvey, drawing a blank form from a drawer in her desk. Dipping a pen in her inkwell, she wrote briefly on the form and sealed it with a gummed label. She wrote an address on the back and pushed it across the blotter to Mrs. Merridge. "Just you take that round to that address. The Gentlemen will see to your last month's wages. I'm not saying anything about a reference, mind you."

Mrs. Merridge stared at the form a long moment before picking it up and departing without a word. Mrs. Corvey exhaled forcefully.

"Bugger," she said. Mrs. Merridge had excelled at making water ices, of which Mrs. Corvey was particularly fond. "Well, can't be helped, I suppose."

Cheered somewhat by the prospect of a month's holiday, Mrs. Corvey rose and locked up her office.

*A*T THE APPOINTED hour next day, the respectable blind widow who lived with her large and remarkably female household at a respectable address sallied forth, family in tow. From the arm of her young son Herbert (in reality Herbertina, in customary male attire) she directed the loading of trunks into a hired carriage, and squeezed in amongst her purported daughters. Herbert hopped up beside the driver, lit up a cigar, and they were off for the railway station!

It was rumored among the Gentlemen (and hence among the Ladies of Nell Gwynne's) that the Society had subterranean tunnels communicating the length and breadth of England; indeed, of Europe itself. However, these were for official business only, if indeed they existed, and the holiday party was obliged to rely upon the technological marvels of the current age.

They thus endured an interesting journey, featuring three separate mechanical breakdowns, on Mr. Isembard Kingdom Brunel's Atmospheric Railway. When they arrived in sunny Torquay, Mrs. Corvey was heard to mutter that being shot from tubes like bleeding champagne corks would never catch on.

A very brief interval afterward, suitably freshened and changed, Mrs. Corvey was seated comfortably on a carriage-rug on the red sands below Beacon Hill, shading herself with a parasol. Jane, Dora and Maude, in identical bathing costumes of blue serge, squealed and splashed happily around the rear steps of a bathing machine. Mrs. Otley wandered the sunny strand, looking for seashells to add to her collection. To one side of Mrs. Corvey, Herbertina sprawled lazily, hat drawn over her eyes. Beyond Herbertina, Miss Rendlesham relaxed with the first volume of *The Tenant of Wildfell Hall*.

At Mrs. Corvey's right hand Lady Beatrice opened her workbag and got out her knitting. It was her custom to make infant garments and present them to charities for poor families. It rather nonplussed the directors of charities that she worked exclusively in scarlet wool, but the infants were not heard to complain.

Midway through a shell-stitch jumper, Lady Beatrice remarked: "I trust I won't offend, Mrs. Corvey, if I ask whether something troubles you?"

Mrs. Corvey, who had been sitting rather stiffly, shrugged. "It's only Mrs. Merridge giving notice as she did. What cooks have against other working women, I'm sure I can't imagine! And it's always so tedious finding a new cook when they've got to get security clearance through the Gentlemen first, and now I shall have to think about that waiting for me at the end of the month."

"Never mind it," said Herbertina, somewhat muffled by her hat. "I'm sure there's enough of us can cook a dish or two ourselves, until we find someone new. Aren't there, girls?"

"I'm certain there are," agreed Lady Beatrice. "I, for example, make a quite passable curried mutton."

"Where'd you learn to make that?" Herbertina tilted her hat back to peer at Lady Beatrice.

"Jellalabad."

"Oh," said Herbertina, and asked nothing further, knowing as she did that Lady Beatrice had survived the Siege of Jellalabad only after surviving the Retreat from Kabul, in which her father's regiment had died to the last man. "Well, I can toast muffins over a fire. You can put quite a lot of things on toasted muffins and make a decent meal. Pilchards. Anchovy relish. You know. I learned that at Eton."

"What were you doing at Eton?" Miss Rendlesham looked up from her novel.

"It's a long story."

Lady Beatrice looked up and down the beach. "We are in a comparatively secluded spot, Mrs. Corvey. Perhaps you'd enjoy trying out the new telescopic function at last?"

"I could do, couldn't I?" Mrs. Corvey brightened. Glancing once over her shoulder, she slipped off her goggles. She then performed a certain muscular contraction (resembling a subdued squint), activating a switch in the brass and crystal apparatus that served her as eyes. With a smooth whirr, the lenses protruded in telescoping sections until they stood a full five inches out from her face. "Oooh! Oh, yes, that's lovely. How close Berry Head looks! And look at all the ships…"

She fell silent, absorbed in watching all the goings-on in the harbor. Fishing boats were coming in, circled by wheeling clouds of crying seabirds. Closer in, the prosperous had moored their yachts, and on each deck was a nearly identical tableau: an industrialist or peer dressed in nautical whites was taking tea in the open air. Each was accompanied by either an overdressed wife and children, a distinctly underdressed young mistress, or a party of fellow yachtsmen. In the last case tea was generally augmented by a great number of bottles.

One late sailor alone was plying the afternoon waters, in a singularly sleek and rakish craft so far out on the horizon it looked half transparent. Mrs. Corvey found herself wondering why he wasn't taking his tea with the others. She watched him a while, and observed that there was something uncertain in the manner in which he was tacking back and forth.

Intrigued, she extended her optics and adjusted the lenses to their highest magnification. The distant yacht leapt at once into close focus, beautifully sharp and clear. It was indeed a trim craft, designed it seemed for racing rather than ostentation. Mrs. Corvey saw three men on deck. Two wore some sort of uniform or livery; the third, clearly the yacht's owner, wore a yachtsman's cap and a startling crimson coat. He stood in the bows, scanning the sea with a spyglass. He seemed to be searching for something.

Mrs. Corvey was speculating idly on whether the fellow might be a latter-day smuggler when she was startled to see something rise from the sea just off the yacht's bow. It resembled a ship's mast, without crosstrees. The yachtsman turned and shouted silently at his helmsman, who took the yacht close to the object. The yachtsman turned and looked toward the shore with what Mrs. Corvey would have sworn was a furtive expression; then turned and hurriedly made his way over the side, down a rope ladder. Mrs. Corvey looked on in astonishment as the yachtsman appeared to walk across the surface of the sea to the mast. He was obscured for a moment by the yacht's bowsprit. When the craft backed again he was nowhere to be seen.

The yacht put about and made off hurriedly, vanishing around Berry Head. The mast appeared to sink straight down into the sea and disappear.

Mrs. Corvey did not surprise easily, as might be imagined, but even so she was a moment in composing herself.

That's got to be something the Gentlemen are working on, she thought. *Must be. Nothing I need to concern myself with on my holidays, to be sure.*

Herbertina stretched her arms wide and yawned. "Well, I'm famished! Do you suppose our tea's ready yet?"

"Oh, I do hope so," said Miss Rendlesham, a little crossly. "Ever since you brought up the subject of muffins, I've been unable to pay attention to my book."

"I could just do with a cup of tea," said Mrs. Corvey thoughtfully, retracting her optics and donning her goggles.

*Y*ET A MERE cream tea, even a substantial one, was unable to make Mrs. Corvey quite forget what she had seen out in the bay. The specter of the mast rising from the sea kept protruding into her thoughts, all through the evening's game of whist and the impromptu song medley the Devere sisters led on the lodging-house's pianoforte. Even the dismal prospect of having to hire a new cook was relegated to the back of Mrs. Corvey's mind by the mystery.

It wasn't so much that anything the Gentlemen's Speculative Society might get up to was capable of surprising her. She knew perfectly well they were always developing technologies both new and arcane, what with their flying machines, steam-powered governess carts and all. It was only that their principal Artificer, Mr. Felmouth, was a single man and rather lonely for conversation, and was in the habit of dropping by Mrs. Corvey's office for a chat over a cup of tea now and then.

On several occasions he had, more or less inadvertently, told her a great deal about projects presently in development. Mrs. Corvey had been obliged to gently remind him about her level of security clearance, and he had apologized with a certain chagrin, but they both understood that any classified information was perfectly safe within the environs of Nell Gwynne's. Mrs. Corvey was fairly sure that if the Gentlemen were testing some sort of underwater craft, she would have heard something about it.

It was shortly after midnight when Mrs. Corvey sat bolt upright in her nightdress, murmuring an oath she had learned at her mother's knee in the workhouse, and climbed from bed. Wrapping a shawl about her shoulders, she opened her trunk and stood before it a moment, indecisive.

She did possess a device appearing to be a sewing-box, which could be reassembled in such a manner as to permit her to transmit an immediate message to the Gentlemen's London headquarters. Did the matter of what she had witnessed require such urgency, however, when it was more than likely to turn out to be some covert field test the Gentlemen themselves were conducting?

Mrs. Corvey drew out her code book instead, and settled down with it at her room's writing desk. The desk was well supplied with paper, ink, pens, sealing-wax, envelopes and postage stamps, as well as a candle in a candlestick. This last item was unnecessary, of course; Mrs. Corvey merely adjusted her optics for night vision as she took pen in hand.

After a half-hour's musing over the codebook, she had composed the following innocent-sounding missive:

> *My very dear Fred,*
> *I take pen in hand to send you best wishes from Torbay. Do you know whether Cousin John decided to come down as well? Caroline is in excellent health. We watched a fisherman pull in the most extraordinary fish. It reminded me of the one we saw at Scotland Yard Wharf. Do write and tell me how you are getting on.*

Translated, this meant:

Attention Fabrication Department.
Level 3 urgency, location Torbay. All well here,
however please confirm whether Field Testing is
conducting maritime operations. Anomaly sighted.
Repeat, please confirm.

Having satisfied her conscience, Mrs. Corvey enclosed
the missive in an envelope, sealed it, addressed it to a particular mail drop location, and affixed a postage stamp. She
set it on the mantelpiece, to be sure of remembering to have
it posted next morning, and retired to her bed, where she
turned off her eyes and slept at last.

*M*RS. CORVEY WAS, as a consequence, a little dull and distracted next morning, but not to such an extent she forgot
to carry her letter down to the dining room. It was sitting
propped against the teapot when Mrs. Otley came down
to breakfast. She was draped with coils of rope, collecting-baskets and a tool belt containing rock hammers in
varying sizes.

"I'm off to Daddyhole, if anyone else would like to go
fossil-hunting," she said hopefully.

There was a resounding silence at the table before Jane,
Dora and Maude spoke together.

"We'd simply love to, only we—"

"I've already put my bathing-costume on under my—"

"I, er, turned my ankle on the path and I don't think—"

"I was just off to the shops for some cigars," said Herbertina. Miss Rendlesham, who had her novel propped open before her plate of kippers and potatoes, simply pretended she hadn't heard.

Seeing Mrs. Otley's downcast expression, Lady Beatrice set aside her napkin. "I believe I'll keep you company, if you wouldn't mind."

"Just post this for me on the way out, would you, dear?" Mrs. Corvey handed her the letter.

"Oh, jolly good!" cried Mrs. Otley. "There are some really splendid Devonian corals, and it is just possible to find an ammonite now and again…"

"…*b*UT ON THE other hand, I once extracted an entire trilobite specimen from calcareous limestone using nothing more than a letter opener and a beefsteak hammer," she was saying after half an hour's steady walking.

"How fascinating," said Lady Beatrice, pausing to disentangle a twig of holm-oak from her hair.

"That was at Lyme, of course," said Mrs. Otley, with a sigh.

"Was that before I signed on? When were we at Lyme?" Lady Beatrice asked in surprise, for Mrs. Corvey was rather pronounced in her preference for Torbay.

"Oh, *we* never were. I lived there once," said Mrs. Otley, and Lady Beatrice nodded discreetly, for it was well understood amongst the ladies that one never inquired directly about a sister whore's past. They walked on a short way, emerging from the wood onto the cliff top, before Mrs. Otley continued: "My father was a scholar, you see, a collector of

natural curiosities. Not, unfortunately, very wise in the ways of the world; after his death I learned the estate was entailed to a third cousin."

"Ah."

"Yes. I had quite a good education, and so I went for a governess, as they say. Unfortunately I was rather unwise in the ways of the world myself, you know, and the usual thing happened."

"I am so sorry to hear it."

"My employer wanted nothing to do with the baby, of course, but I was able to put her out to nurse in the country. It was rather grim for the first two years, providing for her; but after I was recruited, of course, my situation so far improved that I was able to find her a convent school in France."

"How nice."

"Should you like to see her?" Mrs. Otley turned on the path, a little flushed.

"Certainly!"

"Here." Mrs. Otley handed her the collecting-baskets and opened the collar of her bodice. She withdrew a tiny locket and, holding it forth on its chain, opened it to reveal a portrait of an infant. The child had Mrs. Otley's eyes, narrowed in laughter, and tip-tilted nose.

"What a pretty baby!"

"She's quite a young lady now." Self-consciously, Mrs. Otley tucked the locket back out of sight. "Speaks French and writes in a beautiful hand. We correspond, you know. I write as her aunt."

"Of course."

"Well." Mrs. Otley gathered her collecting gear about her again. "Shall we press on? One never knows what the natural erosion will have uncovered. Do you know of Mr. Darwin, the naturalist?"

"I don't believe I do, no."

"Well, he's never been a customer; Royal Society, you know, but he seldom leaves his house at Down. In any case, last year I sent him a specimen of bryozoa and he was kind enough to—"

Both women halted on the path, staring. They had attained the top of the high plain, giving them a splendid view south and eastward across the mild summer sea.

"What on earth is that?" said Lady Beatrice.

"I can't imagine," said Mrs. Otley, shading her eyes with her hand.

They referred to the immense object some distance out, a pale form seeming to hover just under the surface of the water.

"It's far too big to be a whale," said Mrs. Otley.

"And rectangular," said Lady Beatrice.

"Yes, there is that," said Mrs. Otley.

They watched the floating shape for some few minutes. "It doesn't appear to be moving," Mrs. Otley observed.

"Perhaps it is some sort of sunken barge," said Lady Beatrice, just as the thing seemed to lurch in the water and then moved away in the direction of Berry Head, picking up speed as it traveled. "Then again, perhaps not."

The unidentified floating object vanished.

"I think we ought to report to Mrs. Corvey," said Lady Beatrice.

"I quite agree," said Mrs. Otley. "The fossils will still be there tomorrow."

They turned and walked back down the path.

_A_s THEY PASSED the bathing beach, Lady Beatrice noted that although the Devere sisters were once again frolicking in the surf, and Miss Rendlesham had found a shady spot in which to read, Mrs. Corvey was nowhere to be seen. Upon returning to the lodging house, she discovered that this was because Mrs. Corvey had remained in the guests' parlor and was listening, with an expression of patience, to Mrs. Abbott, who had rooms on the second floor.

"...not at all the sort of thing we are accustomed to in these parts," Mrs. Abbott was saying. "In Bonaparte's time there were ever so many alarms about French spies slipping ashore, and of course there are the smugglers, but I really do not know what to make of this, other than that the poor man had been indulging in brandy."

"Have there never been legends of sea monsters before?" Mrs. Corvey inquired.

"Indeed no; one hears tales of them off Scotland and Norway, of course, but then they are such inveterate drinkers in those countries. I suppose it is the beastly cold weather. But one never hears of such things here in *Torquay!*" Mrs. Abbott clicked her knitting needles emphatically.

"How very strange," said Mrs. Corvey. She turned her head in the direction of the parlor door where Lady Beatrice and Mrs. Otley stood. "Has someone just come in?"

"Yes, Mother," said Lady Beatrice. "The sunlight has given Erato a headache, and so we turned back. I hope you'll excuse the question, but has something strange been sighted at sea?"

"That's what Mrs. Abbott here has been telling me," said Mrs. Corvey.

"How very interesting," said Mrs. Otley. "Perhaps you would have the kindness to tell us about it, ma'am?"

"Oh, one of the fishermen has claimed he saw a sea monster," said Mrs. Abbott. "It is all the talk in the taverns; which I only know, of course, because my footman George stepped in for a pot of porter. On the advice of the doctor," she added hastily.

"Of course," said Mrs. Corvey.

"Remarkable," said Lady Beatrice, with a significant lift of her eyebrow.

"I was *told* the man claimed it was a veritable leviathan. He claimed it came up under his fishing smack and struck the hull such a blow that he was nearly thrown into the sea," said Mrs. Abbott, dropping a stitch in her haste to convey the story.

"How fortunate he was not drowned," said Mrs. Otley.

"I should think so," said Mrs. Corvey. "If you will excuse me, Mrs. Abbott—girls, will you just see me upstairs? I believe it's time for Dr. Parry's drops, and you really ought to lie down, Erato dear."

*W*HEN THEY HAD retreated to their rooms, Lady Beatrice and Mrs. Otley lost no time in relating to Mrs. Corvey what they had seen from the cliff top. Mrs. Corvey listened grimly, nodding.

"I saw something of the kind myself, yesterday," she said.

"Do you suppose the Gentlemen are testing something?" said Mrs. Otley.

"That was just what I wrote to enquire," said Mrs. Corvey. "But if it's them, somebody's being bloody careless, because the whole town's talking about 'em. And if it ain't the Gentlemen, then they need to know about it post-haste."

"What ought we to do?" said Lady Beatrice.

"Just what we done," Mrs. Corvey replied. "But if I don't hear back by post soon, I'll be obliged to send to 'em on the Aetheric Transmitter."

A SQUALL OF RAIN blew through in the night, and though it had blown out by morning, the sands were unpleasantly chilly and damp. As a consequence, rather than go bathing, the ladies went for a stroll along Victoria Parade to look in the shop windows.

They trooped along together, enjoying the splendid views across the bay, to say nothing of the unaccustomed fresh air and sunlight, until misfortune overtook them. It chanced that

Miss Rendlesham had had a bonnet of a whimsical nature trimmed up especially for the seaside. Rather than the customary silk roses or violets, it was adorned with a cockade incorporating several real seashells, a dried seahorse, and a shrimp made from oiled paper and painted plaster, the latter very lifelike. Far too lifelike, as they discovered whilst idling outside a confectioner's shop window.

"Look out!" cried Lady Beatrice, who had glanced up just in time to see a gull swooping down. The others screamed and ducked as the bird beat its wings wildly, striking and pulling at the faux prawn. Miss Rendlesham cowered, clutching the ribbons by which her bonnet was held on. Herbertina had just taken Mrs. Corvey's cane and was aiming a blow at the importunate bird when something flashed overhead and impacted the gull. There was an explosion of feathers, and an inordinately huge knife bounced off Miss Rendlesham' shoulder and landed with a clatter on the paving. The gull squawked once and veered off, flopping into the sea.

There was a renewed chorus of screams (and an oath from Herbertina). Miss Rendlesham stood trembling in a cloud of feathers, afraid to let go of her hat. Mrs. Corvey snatched her cane back from Herbertina and gingerly poked at the knife. "Dear God, is someone chucking cutlasses around here?"

"Ma'am!" cried a male voice, and looking up they beheld a man running toward them along the seafront.

"I believe this is our knight errant," said Lady Beatrice, observing him closely as he neared them. He was a tall and well-built gentleman in a light summer suit, with a fine head of chestnut curls and prodigious whiskers. As he came close enough to look into Lady Beatrice's eyes he halted and pulled himself up, in an effect remarkably similar to a stallion rearing. Lady Beatrice sighed inwardly. She often had that effect on men. She assumed it was due to her eyes, which were grey and had a rather penetrating gaze.

"I—I—Ma'am, I must h'apologize for the h'intrusion, but I saw the young lady being h'assailed—and I, ah…" The gentleman's booming voice, which bespoke the American South despite his music hall accent, trailed away as he stared at Lady Beatrice, his mouth slightly open.

"It was very good of you," she told him. He remained gaping at her, apparently spellbound, a moment longer before recollecting himself and bending to scoop up the knife. He returned the knife to his inside coat pocket, and belatedly removed his hat.

"Forgive my, ah, I mean, we 'aven't been h'introduced— Allow me to—the name's Tredway Pickett, ma'am." Mr. Pickett seized Lady Beatrice's hand and bent over it in a fervent kiss.

"How do you do, Mr. Pickett," murmured Lady Beatrice.

"I do 'ope the young lady wasn't too scared by me knife? I do think I got the villainous creature," said Mr. Pickett, straightening up but not relinquishing Lady Beatrice's hand.

"You did, Mr. Pickett, without question. Were you much frightened, Charlotte?" Lady Beatrice turned to regard Miss Rendlesham.

"Only moderately," replied Miss Rendlesham, who had taken off her bonnet and was regarding it in some chagrin. "More by that dreadful great knife than by the gull!"

"Ah, that's a Bowie knife," beamed Mr. Pickett. "H'ive killed bears with that knife, ma'am—a little bird like that was no problem h'at all."

"Bears? What's happened, Beatrice dear?" said Mrs. Corvey, pointedly looking in the wrong direction.

"Do not upset yourself, Mamma. The bear is, I am sure, only a figure of speech. A bird attacked Charlotte's bonnet, and this kind gentleman came to our aid. He threw a knife at it, which was a little alarming but certainly timely aid," said Lady Beatrice diplomatically. "Ah—Mr. Pickett, may I present my mother, Mrs. Elizabeth Corvey?"

"Charmed, ma'am," said Mr. Pickett, taking her hand and brushing it with his mustache.

"And let me introduce my brother Herbert; my sisters Jane, Dora and Maude; and my cousins Erato Otley and Charlotte Rendlesham," said Lady Beatrice.

"Charmed, ladies; sir. And you must be Miss Beatrice Corvey, ma'am?" said Mr. Pickett hopefully. Lady Beatrice made a graceful gesture of acknowledgment.

"I am, sir."

"Well. I must say, Miss Beatrice, I'm 'eartily sorry for the h'inconvenience to your fair cousin, but delighted on me own h'account to meet so many h'enchanting ladies. As it 'appens, I'm throwing a ball tonight, a sort of welcome event, you know, and the guest list was a little short on h'account of me not knowing too many of the gentry 'ereabouts yet. Perhaps you ladies would care to h'attend?"

"Oh, Mamma, might we?" cried Dora, clasping her hands. Their vocation being what it was, the ladies seldom got invited to parties in a non-professional capacity. And after all, they were on holiday.

"I assure you, ma'am, all proprieties will be h'observed," said Mr. Pickett.

"I haven't danced in simply ages," said Maude.

"I suppose it wouldn't hurt," said Mrs. Corvey. Her black lenses were now fixed on Mr. Pickett. "It is a little irregular, but we are on holiday, after all."

"Gor blimey! That'd be simply fine, ma'am," said Mr. Pickett, taking her hand once again and shaking it heartily. "It's right over yonder there at the Royal, at 9 o'clock. I would be delighted to send a carriage for you."

"Nonsense, young man," said Mrs. Corvey firmly. "We're staying quite close at hand. The walk will do my young ladies good."

"I look forward to seeing you then." Mr. Pickett replaced his hat. "There won't be h'any trouble with h'invitations at the door; just you tell them Mr. Tredway Pickett said you all were h'invited."

"Most gracious, I'm sure," said Mrs. Corvey.

"I will not h'impede your perambulation any further, then," said Mr. Pickett, tipping his hat. "Ladies. Sir. Miss Beatrice."

He strode away from them along the Parade. They watched him go, somewhat bemused.

"'Gor blimey'?" said Mrs. Otley.

"The man is obviously an American. Why on earth does he effect that...astonishing accent?" returned Miss Rendlesham in faint horror.

"Why indeed?" said Mrs. Corvey; but what she was most urgently wondering to herself was: why and how had the peculiar American stepped off his yacht into the sea the previous day? Because she was almost certain he was the man she had observed from the beach.

*T*HAT AFTERNOON A letter arrived from London, bearing the innocuous return address the Gentlemen employed for correspondence. The landlady presented it to Herbertina, who thanked her and bore it straight upstairs to Mrs. Corvey. Its text, when decrypted, read as follows:

> *Regarding yours of the 2nd: no field trials being conducted in your area. Please send more detailed account using Encryption 7.*

Upon reading this, Mrs. Corvey sighed, rummaged through her trunk for the encryption book and settled down to write a long and detailed letter.

*T*HE ROYAL HOTEL stood prominently at the intersection of Victoria Parade and The Strand, and was therefore an easy five minutes' walk from the Ladies' lodging house. The windows blazed with light as they approached and a great many people milled about the entrance, peering in; for balls were an infrequent occurrence in Torquay, given that so many of its visitors were invalids hoping to restore their health.

A gentleman of indeterminate status, in a powdered wig, bowed them across the threshold and directed them inward. They were able to find their own way to the ballroom, following the strains of "Sir Roger de Coverly", and on entering beheld a grand salon with walls painted in the Etruscan style and no less than three chandeliers casting their blazing light on what must be admitted to be a rather poor turnout. Some four or five couples were doing their best to comprise a set as

Mr. Pickett watched gloomily from beside the punch bowl. His face brightened immeasurably, however, when he spotted Lady Beatrice.

"Miss Beatrice!" he said, easily audible over the orchestra, as he advanced upon her. "And your charming family. I am delighted, ma'am, just delighted that you all could h'attend. Ma'am, may I h'offer you a cup of punch?" he said to Mrs. Corvey as he more or less swept her off to a chair by the wall.

"Too kind," murmured Mrs. Corvey.

"Waiter! A cup of punch for the lady!" bawled Mr. Pickett. Turning to Herbertina, he said: "There's a bar right through that door yonder, with cigars and brandy, sir, if you're so disposed."

"Oh, jolly good," said Herbertina in relief.

"And I reckon this thing is h'about bloody done—" Mr. Pickett looked over his shoulder at the Roger de Coverly set, which was coming to its anticlimactic close. "There! I thought they'd 'ave to get it over with sooner or later. Hi! Give us a waltz next," he ordered the orchestra.

They obliged promptly. He bowed to Lady Beatrice. "Miss Beatrice, may I 'ave the honor of this dance?"

Lady Beatrice extended her hand and found herself borne out onto the dance floor. She had not danced since her days in Simla, and was at first concerned lest she display some clumsiness on that account. She soon saw that she need have no fears, Mr. Pickett proving so domineering a partner that she might as well have been a dressmaker's dummy on wheels.

As they whirled around, Lady Beatrice glimpsed some of the gentlemen guests eagerly approaching the newcomers;

who, with fluttering fans and demurely downcast eyes, were giving a formidable imitation of respectable debutantes. Herbertina, on the other hand, appeared to have been ambushed in her progress to the bar by a number of hopeful females, and was looking extremely annoyed at being obliged to do the gentlemanly thing and ask one of them to dance.

"May I just say, Miss Beatrice, you look h'exceptionally lovely this h'evening? 'Ow seldom it is one finds oneself in the company of one so h'exquisitely refined," Mr. Pickett shouted over the music.

"Thank you. Mr. Pickett, surely you are an American?"

He looked crestfallen. "Aw. You smoked me, then?"

"The—Bowie knife, was it? That was quite distinctive, Mr. Pickett," Lady Beatrice said with some understatement, "and your voice does betray a certain hint of the Southern areas of America."

"I thought I had the lingo down pat. And here I've been paying that butler good money to teach me the accents of the mother tongue," said Mr. Pickett, growing somewhat redder in the face than even his vigorous dancing might have induced.

Lady Beatrice quelled an urge to laugh. "They are correct for the East End, I believe, but not really suitable for a gentleman of your station. Your...natural accent is quite charming."

Mr. Pickett scowled. "If he's been having fun at my expense, I'll make him wish he hadn't. See, the truth is, Miss Beatrice—I *am* English, by blood and descent. The Picketts were cavaliers who left for America when Oliver Cromwell was running things over here. They should have gone back home after things were set to rights, but they didn't, somehow. They stayed on in America, which was a fatal mistake. It's no country for gentlemen, that is for certain sure."

"I have heard that opinion expressed," said Lady Beatrice cautiously.

"Well, I'm here to tell you it's true. I have turned my back forever on the land of my nativity and returned to the mother country! What kind of a nation is it, I ask you, that puts a miserable county tax assessor in a position to insult a man of quality? With impunity too, may I say, because you just can't demand satisfaction of that kind of low-born churl."

"I am so sorry to hear it, Mr. Pickett," said Lady Beatrice, noting the red glare in his eyes as he worked himself into a rage. She predicted he would gnash his teeth next, and was obscurely pleased with herself when he did so.

"Varlets! That is just exactly the word for what they are, Miss Beatrice. A whole nation of varlets. I will not dismay you with an account of the circumstances of my departure; I will only say I suffered intolerable abuse at the hands of petty tyrants. No, I'm well rid of America and pleased as punch to be back on my *true* ancestral soil. I want nothing more than to become as one hundred per cent an Englishman outwardly as I am in my heart."

"What a noble goal," said Lady Beatrice, thinking to herself that it was going to be a long evening.

MRS. CORVEY SAT in her appointed chair against the wall, sipping from her cup of punch and watching the dancers. The waltz ended; couples disengaged, bowed or curtsied, and most made for the punchbowl. Mr. Pickett showed no signs of relinquishing Lady Beatrice, however. He called for a galop, the orchestra struck up a lively tune, and Mr. Pickett and Lady Beatrice went speeding away down the dance floor. A pair of misses settled down two chairs from Mrs. Corvey, fanning themselves energetically.

"Well!" said one of the young ladies. "Mamma won't be pleased. He seems quite taken by that minx in the red gown."

"She's welcome to him," said the other young lady with a shudder. "He really is the most frightful eccentric!"

"I thought I should die laughing at that accent!"

The other miss leaned toward her friend, and in what was presumably her best imitation of stern matronly tones said: "But, my dear, he's as rich as Croesus!"

"There is that," said the first young lady. "Tabby says he's paid a year's lease on Waldon House."

"A year's lease! Fancy living here year-round. He isn't going up to London for the season?"

"I don't believe he is aware of our customs," said her friend primly. "Why are the rich ones always complete barbarians? Mamma said that she heard he intends to buy the land along the cliff tops by St. Mary's Bay, because he wishes to build a mansion there."

"Fancy anyone wanting to live over there with no Society but the sheep!"

"Clearly he is of a romantic nature," said the one. The other rolled her eyes and they lifted their fans to discreetly mask their giggles.

At this point Mrs. Corvey spotted Herbertina emerging from the bar in a cloud of cigar smoke. She hurried to the punch table, ladled herself a drink, and took a seat beside Mrs. Corvey.

"My God, he's smitten with her, isn't he?" she said, nodding her head in the direction of Lady Beatrice and Mr. Pickett.

"Seems to be," said Mrs. Corvey.

"Several fellows were discussing him in the bar," said Herbertina. "They're all sick with envy for his racing yacht. Designed her himself, someone said. I gather she's won three races already. *The Sceptre*, I think they said she's called."

"Anyone know why he talks like a Stepney greengrocer?" said Mrs. Corvey.

"People assume he's a bit mad, though they agree he's brilliant at ship building," said Herbertina with a shrug. She reached into her waistcoat pocket and felt about. "Damn! I left my lucifer case in the bar." She rose hastily and went off in search of it.

THE GALOP IS not normally a conversational dance, since so much effort is required simply to breathe while dancing. However, even storming through it like a wild mustang of the Western plains as he did, Mr. Pickett's lungs proved equal to the challenge.

"I must say, Miss Beatrice, *you* speak in a splendidly refined manner," he roared. "Would you be at all agreeable to giving me elocution lessons? I'd pay handsomely."

It was a moment before Lady Beatrice could reply, caught as she was between astonishment and the need to inhale. Mr. Pickett, watching her face closely, went red once more.

"Miss Beatrice, I must apologize! I certainly intended no offense. I hope you'll forgive a poor scion of Britain raised among ruder stock," he implored.

"Quite," said Lady Beatrice, as the music thudded to its conclusion. "Mr. Picket, I confess I am somewhat fatigued. Might I be escorted to a chair?"

"*W*OULD YOU BE at all inclined to some liquid refreshment, Miss Beatrice?" said Mr. Pickett as he bowed her to her seat by Mrs. Corvey, who sat presently alone, dance partners having claimed all the other staff of Nell Gwynne's for a stately quadrille.

"That would be most kind." Lady Beatrice opened her fan and fluttered it in a not-quite-dismissive manner to speed Mr. Pickett on his way.

"Your cheeks are pink and your pupils are dilated," observed Mrs. Corvey. "Having a good time, are we?"

"An energetic one, at least. I would appear to have an admirer," said Lady Beatrice. "It appears that Mr. Pickett desires to alter himself into an Englishman, and has been led astray in this enterprise by his butler. Evidently he was convinced that bizarre accent was correct."

"Hears what he wants to hear and then believes it, I dare say," commented Mrs. Corvey.

Lady Beatrice, remembering the glaring eyes and gnashing teeth, nodded thoughtfully.

"He is understandably unhappy with the results, now. Do you know, he asked me to give him elocution lessons? And then was struck with mortification when he realized he had offered me money."

"Money, eh?" Mrs. Corvey suppressed a chuckle. "What a thoughtful gentleman, to be sure. Well, I should tell him *Yes* to those elocution lessons, my dear."

"Truly?" Lady Beatrice glanced sidelong at Mrs. Corvey.

"Oh, yes. I think our Mr. Pickett bears watching," said Mrs. Corvey, just as that gentleman returned and presented Lady Beatrice with a cup of punch.

"Sweets to the sweet, and refreshment to one who refreshes all eyes," he said, with a gallant bow.

"Thank you so much, dear Mr. Pickett," said Lady Beatrice. "Mamma has agreed that it would be quite proper to assist you in learning more suitable accents. My only fee, of course, shall be that Mamma be permitted to attend us and so partake of the restorative air for which Torbay is so well known."

"Indeed, young man," said Mrs. Corvey, gazing at a spot some two feet to the left of Mr. Pickett.

Mr. Pickett grinned hugely. "Why, certainly," he said with a broad wink at Lady Beatrice. "Mother shall certainly come along as a chaperone. When may I call upon you, and at what o'clock, Miss Beatrice and Mrs. Corvey? I have a fine four-in-hand and we can take in something of the countryside."

"Perhaps the day after tomorrow, in the early afternoon," said Mrs. Corvey. "My girls are late sleepers."

*N*EXT DAY, AS shortly after midday as could possible be construed to be "early afternoon," a messenger with a gift called upon Lady Beatrice. She and Mrs. Corvey went downstairs to the lodging house parlor to receive it.

The messenger was a man in good new suit that in no way disguised his dubious origins. His face bore a notably crooked nose, and his hands were calloused and bent into permanent half-open fists; despite which, a fine gold ring gleamed on the right one. His voice was a pleasant tenor with a much better-bred accent that the unfortunate Mr. Pickett; however, his half-smile and bold gaze quite gave the lie to his obsequious tone. Also, he leered at Lady Beatrice.

Introducing himself as Mr. Felan, "Mr. Pickett's man," he was well-spoken enough as he proffered Mr. Pickett's compliments and a lovely Chinoiserie vase full of scarlet roses.

"Mr. Pickett said to tell you, ma'am," Felan said in mockserious tones to Mrs. Corvey, "that he sent the flower of his gardens to the flower of yours."

Lady Beatrice took the vase. "What lovely roses! They are very fine, Mamma."

"How thoughtful," Mrs. Corvey replied icily. "Please convey our thanks to Mr. Pickett. Beatrice, do help me back upstairs now."

Being apparently blind did mean she never had to pay much attention to other people's reactions, and she was pleased to turn her shoulder on Pickett's man and return back up the stairs. His face fell and his smile twisted rather nastily as she and Beatrice departed—of course, as Mrs. Corvey was most emphatically not really blind, she was also able to see and note this alteration in his demeanor.

"An impudent servant; and a nasty piece of work, I shouldn't wonder," she said to Lady Beatrice as they passed the first landing. "And a boxer once, I think—did you note the fellow's hands?"

"I did. They have seen hard usage," said Lady Beatrice.

"And dealt it out, I've no doubt. That sort often goes for a bully-boy, once they get too slow for the ring," said Mrs.

Corvey. "Reminds me of one of Lord Brougham's followers, was a bit of an enforcer in that to-do back in '45 about changing the Coroner's Laws; you may recall, there was quite a bit of resurrectionist scandal then."

"I believe I heard of it," said Lady Beatrice. She followed Mrs. Corvey into their suite.

"We entertained the fellow on his master's business a few times," continued Mrs. Corvey, "when it was a matter of some concern to the Gentlemen that there might be a resurrectionist ring attached to Lord Brougham's household."

"And was there? Was he indeed a resurrectionist?" Lady Beatrice asked with interest, setting the vase on a table where the roses caught the light.

"O, yes, some little business deal between the Lord's wine steward, this bully cove and the College of Surgeons; all manner of mischief in their respective cellars…but Mr. Pickett's man brought him to mind because he had just that same manner of speaking you soft and yet being snarky. And he was very rough with the girls, especially Erato. I finally had to remove him."

Mrs. Corvey, having shed her gloves and shawl, settled down in the armchair by the table. Lady Beatrice, arranging the roses to best show in the sunlight, gazed at her a little moment.

"How did you have him removed, if I may ask?" she inquired finally.

"Shot the bugger in the head and had him dumped in the Thames," said Mrs. Corvey with a reminiscent smile. She looked sharply at Beatrice, her lenses whirring to a close focus. "You watch yourself around that one, Beatrice. His master may be a Southern gentleman, but our Mr. Felan is a wolf."

Lady Beatrice nodded. "I shall do so."

"Wear your garter knife, then," Mrs. Corvey said with an air of maternal authority; and leaned back in her chair with a worried frown.

 PRECISELY HALF-PAST one the following afternoon, a boy from the front desk knocked on the door of their suite, and informed the ladies that Mr. Pickett had arrived for their outing.

"Mind you get him talking as much as ever you can," Mrs. Corvey said to Lady Beatrice, to whom she had explained her suspicions.

"I don't believe that will prove difficult," said Lady Beatrice as they entered the boarding house's parlor.

It was certainly not difficult to spot Mr. Pickett where he waited by the front door. He was attired in a coat of brilliant crimson with lace at the throat and cuffs; it confirmed Mrs. Corvey's tentative identification of him as the water-walking yachtsman she had seen. Though the rest of his clothing was fairly sober, it could not offset the effect of the coat, which made Mr. Pickett look rather like a pantomime highwayman. He strode forward, seized Lady Beatrice's hand, and kissed it resoundingly.

"Your chariot awaits, Miss Beatrice," said Mr. Pickett. "Your servant, Mrs. Corvey, ma'am. Let us take the salubrious air."

He led them out to what was in fact an open barouche, drawn by four fine bays. He had evidently come alone, acting as his own driver. Mrs. Corvey was deposited within the carriage; Lady Beatrice was handed up to the driver's seat, into which Mr. Pickett vaulted a moment later. They set off, taking the beach road south.

They drove first to Tor Abbey, admiring what could be seen of its stately ruins while Mr. Pickett discoursed at length and with admiration on Henry VIII's dissolution of the monasteries.

"It takes a good strong-willed Englishman to stand up to the Pope," announced Mr. Pickett.

He further pointed out the antique barn in which Sir Francis Drake had imprisoned a quantity of Spaniards following the Armada. Thereafter he spoke for some time on the subject of Britain's naval glory, with Lady Beatrice managing to interject the occasional "Quite" or "Really?" all the way to the unbearably quaint village of Cockington. At the sight of its thatched roofs and mellow brick there were positive tears in Mr. Pickett's eyes, and he spoke for a quarter-hour straight on the rural charms of Devon.

"In just such a village," he cried, "the great Sir Francis Drake would have been born. There's a hero for you! Circumnavigated the globe, and brought honor and glory to his native land. They don't breed 'em like that nowadays."

"He is a particular hero of yours, then, " said Lady Beatrice.

"Oh, indeed, Miss Beatrice, ma'am! And, if you will excuse the opinion of a poor Colonial returned to the fold, I do think it's a sin and a shame our present Queen hasn't men like that running *her* Navy."

"How true," remarked Lady Beatrice, with a glance back at Mrs. Corvey.

Mr. Pickett continued loud in his praises of Drake, all the way through Paignton, Broadsands, Churston Ferrers and was still going when they reached Brixham. It became obvious he had read a great deal on the subject of Drake, as well as Hawkins, Raleigh, and other gentlemen mariners and privateers. At least he had abandoned his "English" accent.

As they idled along the green cliff tops above St. Mary's Bay, Lady Beatrice seized upon the opportunity afforded by Mr. Pickett pausing to draw breath and said: "Are not you yourself a mariner, Mr. Pickett? Some of our fellow lodgers have spoken with admiration of your yacht."

Mr. Pickett blushed a bit but looked pleased. "Well, I don't like to brag, but the old *Sceptre* is a mighty fine boat. I may have won one or two prizes with her; they're back at the house. The place I'm staying, I mean." He waved a hand at the open expanse of bluffs, that were empty save for three tiny cottages huddled together. "Look there, Miss Beatrice; wouldn't that make a fine spot for an elegant residence? You can't beat the view, can you?"

"It is certainly impressive," said Lady Beatrice.

Mr. Pickett reined in the horses and the barouche came to a gentle halt. Sitting there above what genuinely was a spectacular view of the Bay, Mr. Pickett edged a little closer to Lady Beatrice and resumed his elucidation upon the glories of English military victories of the 16th century, presenting them to Lady Beatrice under the evident impression that she had never heard of these things and would be edified to learn of them. Lady Beatrice, who had grown up in a soldier's household, smiled, murmured polite remarks and now and then raised an eyebrow for his benefit. She had been asked to feign ignorance of much stranger things in a professional capacity.

Mrs. Corvey, forgotten behind them, watched with interest as a man in a workman's clothes emerged from one of the three cottages. He looked up at Mr. Pickett with obvious recognition and started forward across the cliff top, apparently intending to speak with him. Having covered slightly less than half the distance, however, he seemed to notice Lady Beatrice's presence and halted in his tracks. He watched uncertainly for several minutes before seemingly changing his mind and hurrying back to the cottages, glancing several times over his shoulder on his way. Within the shading edge of her bonnet, Mrs. Corvey's lenses turned just enough to bring the face of none other than Mr. Felan into focus. Having noted this well, Mrs. Corvey nodded thoughtfully and returned her attention to Mr. Pickett's monologue.

Keen and fixed though her attention was, she nevertheless became conscious of a certain distraction, now that the carriage was motionless; a sort of thrilling vibration emanating upward, it seemed, though the very wheels. And was there a certain hollow musicality in the boom of the surf?

"Are you quite all right, Mamma?" inquired Lady Beatrice; who, on glancing back at her, had noted Mrs. Corvey's puzzled scowl.

"Oh, quite all right, my dear; only I was thinking there's such a funny noise to the sea hereabouts," said Mrs. Corvey.

"Why, that would be the caves," said Mr. Pickett. "Lots of sea-caves here, ma'am."

"Sea-caves, to be sure," said Mrs. Corvey. "Thank you, young man."

*P*ROFUSE AS HE had been with his praises for the British on the ride out to St. Mary's Bay, on the return journey Mr.

Picket focused his admiration on Lady Beatrice in specific, although in a gentlemanly manner. The subject of elocution lessons was once again raised. Lady Beatrice obligingly set about correcting his vowel sounds and encouraging a greater crispness in his native drawl.

Upon returning to Torquay, Mr. Pickett insisted that they take tea with him, an offer Mrs. Corvey accepted with enthusiasm.

"It's a nice place, but a little too modern for my tastes," said Mr. Pickett, leading them up the walk of an ostentatiously grand house of recent construction. "I confess to being a man of old-fashioned preferences. It'll do until I can build myself something better, though." He drew a key from his pocket and let them in himself. "Service may be a little slow today; I gave that butler a piece of my mind and sent him packing this morning. No man makes a fool of Tredway Pickett, no sir."

He led them into a splendidly airy parlor with a view of the sea. It was, however, somewhat sparsely furnished; Lady Beatrice and Mrs. Corvey perched together on the single low settee, while Mr. Pickett dragged close an occasional table and set it before them. Having retrieved a chair from the desk in the far corner of the room, he sat opposite the ladies and bawled: "Alfred!"

A moment later, a footman appeared in the doorway, showing a certain reluctance. "Alfred, kindly take the ladies' bonnets and cloaks, and tell Mrs. Drumm I want her finest tea for three persons."

"Very good, sir."

Mr. Pickett entertained them with light conversation on the subject of his yachting triumphs, pointing with pride to the trophies on the mantelpiece, until tea was duly brought in by the cook and housemaid. The dainties arranged upon the tray—tiny sandwiches, petits fours and buns—looked delicious; but the cook (in keeping with the fierce temper implied by her fading red hair) glared so balefully at Mr. Pickett as she set them out that Mrs. Corvey half-expected them to be laced with arsenic. *Cook's unhappy in her situation,* thought Mrs. Corvey to herself. She watched thoughtfully as Mrs. Drumm departed the room in highest dudgeon, and an oblivious Mr. Pickett talked on.

"...and, by jingo, it worked, because I shot past him and the scoundrel ran himself on a sandbar! I always say, when a gentleman goes in for a sport, he ought to play to win," said Mr. Pickett. He noticed the teapot, looked uneasily from Mrs. Corvey to Lady Beatrice, and at last made up his mind. "Ah—Miss Beatrice, ma'am, I believe it would be correct to ask you to do the pouring?"

"I should be delighted," said Lady Beatrice smoothly.

Tea was served round, and Mrs. Corvey was elated to discover that, whatever animus the cook might bear her master, it did not influence her culinary performance; at least as far as cress sandwiches and tiny cakes were concerned. *Wonder if she can do water ices,* Mrs. Corvey speculated.

"I hope this meets with you ladies' approval," said Mr. Pickett. "Fine old English custom, afternoon tea."

"It is really quite pleasant, Mr. Pickett," Lady Beatrice assured him. He positively beamed at her. She took a long, slow sip of tea, keeping her eyes fixed steadily on his, and was interested to note the color rise in his face.

Mrs. Corvey noted it also.

"Why—thank you, ma'am," said Mr. Picket.

"You are most welcome, dear Mr. Pickett. Do you not find that the sea air gives one a prodigious appetite?" said Lady Beatrice. Still holding his gaze, she sank her white teeth into a bun.

Mr. Pickett coughed. "I do indeed, Miss Beatrice."

During the ensuing conversation, through which Mr. Pickett was unable to tear his eyes from the slow progression of delicacies towards Lady Beatrice's red lips, Mrs. Corvey grew silent and at last unobtrusively set her cup and saucer to one side. Composing herself in a comfortable attitude, she feigned sleep. Lady Beatrice, who had been half-expecting this development, glanced sideways at her and spoke in a lowered voice to Mr. Pickett.

"Oh! Dear Mamma has fallen asleep. Perhaps it is the unaccustomed exercise." She set down her own cup and saucer on the depleted tea tray. "Let us not disturb her. Have you anywhere private wherein we may continue our conversation, Mr. Pickett? A garden, perhaps?"

"Why, there is indeed a garden, Miss Beatrice," Mr. Pickett whispered loudly, rising and offering her his arm. "Your servant, ma'am!"

Lady Beatrice rose, took his arm, and with serene and unshakeable purpose led him out upon the terrace.

Mrs. Corvey, once well-assured of privacy, rose and swiftly approached the roll top desk at the far end of the room. She was pleased to see the desk was open and unlocked, rendering her set of lock picks unnecessary. Rapidly she sorted through the papers scattered here and there on the desk.

They consisted principally of receipts and bills of trade from wholesale dealers in iron and steel, timber, and chemicals of the sort most commonly used in the manufacture of incendiary devices; all of which Mr. Pickett appeared to have purchased in remarkably large quantities. There was also a long list of accounts of what appeared to be wages paid to laborers, as well as pages of extensive correspondence with a Mr. Shrove, who seemed to operate a foundry.

In addition to these, Mrs. Corvey found some rather heated correspondence with an American banking house, contrasting with rather more cordial letters of inquiry to one Mr. Lawrence, a house agent. Mr. Pickett certainly seemed well-supplied with funds, and determined to stay in England.

Nothing more of importance was to be found, though Mrs. Corvey searched diligently, and long before she heard approaching footsteps had returned to the settee. She watched sidelong as Mrs. Drumm, accompanied by the housemaid, peered into the room.

"Looks like they've finished," the housemaid murmured.

Mrs. Corvey sat upright and in her sweetest and most tremulous voice called out: "Is someone there?"

Mrs. Drumm cleared her throat. "Shall we take away the tea things, madam?"

"Indeed, I think you might," said Mrs. Corvey.

She watched as Mrs. Drumm and her fellow domestic entered the room and began clearing away the trays. Mrs. Drumm, thinking herself unseen, pointed at the remaining watercress sandwiches and elbowed the housemaid.

"Look at that! Always asks for 'em and scarcely touches 'em!," she muttered, apparently under the impression that Mrs. Corvey was deaf as well as blind.

"What was that, my dear?" inquired Mrs. Corvey, putting her hand to her ear.

"I was only wondering, madam, whether the cress sandwiches was all right," said Mrs. Drumm with a sniff.

"Oh, I had two, myself," exclaimed Mrs. Corvey, clasping her hands. "They were delightful. And I quite enjoyed the buns and tea cakes. Your pastry cook, if I may say so, is an artist, my dear, a positive artist."

Mrs. Drumm's ruddy face brightened still further with pleasure. "Very kind of you to say so, madam, I'm sure, as it was me in fact made 'em."

"What a fortunate man your employer is," replied Mrs. Corvey.

The maid made a disgruntled noise and Mrs. Drumm shot her a warning glance. Mrs. Corvey, observing this, inquired delicately, "I wonder whether I might ask if you are content in your situation, Mrs. Drumm?"

"I'm sure I could speak no ill of him what pays my wages, madam," said Mrs. Drumm in a tone which implied exactly the opposite.

"Of course," said Mrs. Corvey in a tone which implied *she* understood exactly what Mrs. Drumm meant. "On the other hand, any sensible woman with a splendid gift must surely be sensitive to opportunities for advancement."

Mrs. Drumm eyed her in silence for a moment. Her eyes were as black as Mrs. Corvey's own, if more natural, but gave her examining stare a considerable sharpness. Turning to the housemaid, she said, "Dolly, just you get them trays downstairs."

"What, both of them?" said Dolly querulously.

Mrs. Drumm appropriated the plate of sandwiches and hurriedly stacked the trays one upon another. "There! Take 'em off."

Dolly complied sulkily as Mrs. Drumm took the liberty of seating herself opposite Mrs. Corvey. "May I offer you another sandwich, madam?"

"Oh, were there any more? I was sure they had all been ate up," said Mrs. Corvey, groping forward. Mrs. Drumm passed her a sandwich and took one herself. Mrs. Corvey consumed hers with sounds of dignified rapture; Mrs. Drumm looked pleased.

"I make an excellent cucumber sandwich, as well," she said.

"*So* refreshing in the summertime," exclaimed Mrs. Corvey. "I don't suppose you have a receipt for water ices?"

"It happens I do, madam," replied Mrs. Drumm. "Water ices, ice cream bombes, syllabubs, panachee jellies, flummeries, and fancy ice water cups."

Mrs. Corvey contained herself. "I should have thought you might have commanded your own price in London," she said diffidently.

"Saving your grace, I should have thought so too," said Mrs. Drumm with a shrug, helping herself to another sandwich. "But times is hard and you take what you can."

"You understand, I hope, that I ask simply because Mr. Pickett and my daughter seem to get on very well—is he an agreeable employer?" said Mrs. Corvey.

Mrs. Drumm grimaced.

"Can't tell a lie, madam, I've never worked for such a man. He's that given to temper—last night he came in roaring and fired poor Mr. Ponsonby, saying he'd made him look a fool. Nearly hit him with his walking stick! I suspect that's the way they carry on in America, but it won't do here. And this morning everything was sixes and sevens and who's to run the household, I'd like to know? Tells me he wants all kinds of real

English food—but he won't touch the suet pudding, won't touch the mutton, won't touch the boiled beef and carrots, and only picks at the roast chicken and sends it back, asking whether I don't know how to fry it! And when I fries it as best I can, with a nice bit of gammon on the side, he says it still ain't right."

"Dear me, how dreadful," said Mrs. Corvey. "I think this would prove rather a trial for my daughter. If you will pardon the indelicacy, Mrs. Drumm, he must pay you frightfully well, if you are willing to endure such a difficult master."

"Not all that well," said Mrs. Drumm grimly, eying the last sandwich on the plate.

"And if some other party was to offer you a situation?"

"It would be duly considered, madam." Having decided against eating the last sandwich, Mrs. Drumm rose to her feet, took the dish and stopped midway through a curtsey, concluding that there was no point when her knees hurt and she was addressing a blind woman anyway. "I do beg your pardon, madam, but I ought to get back to the kitchen."

*M*R. PICKETT HAD apparently not found occasion to quarrel with his gardener. His garden lawn was immaculately sheared in perfect geometric stripes and the hedges shielding the garden from his neighbors were well-tended, vigorous, and gratifyingly tall, providing more than adequate concealment for any strolling couple.

"It is a splendid sea view, Miss Beatrice, is it not?" said Mr. Pickett, hopefully slipping his arm around Lady Beatrice's waist. To his great relief, she did not stiffen or withdraw, but rather responded to the liberty with supple compliance.

"It is an enthralling view," said Lady Beatrice, looking deeply into his eyes.

"I reckon the house I'm proposing to build will have a view that beats this one, all the same," said Mr. Pickett a little breathlessly, for Lady Beatrice's steady grey gaze was having a distinct effect on his vascular system.

"I am sure it shall," said Lady Beatrice. She somehow managed to sway closer, so that the cloud-like silk of her skirts frothed about his legs.

Experiencing a frisson of irrational happiness, Mr. Pickett continued:

"A fine view, a fine house in every way. I'm not planning to throw up any little bachelor shack, you understand, Miss Beatrice: I'm intending a real old proper British mansion with room for generations to come. A place where a man might settle down, take a gracious lady to wife, and raise a brood of valiant Englishmen, like a nest of sea-eagles, ever-ready to defend their mother country from vile invaders. Why, nothing would please me more than that our dearly beloved future monarchs might rest confident in the knowledge that as long as the Picketts of Devon live, England's shores will be safe."

"How noble; how brave," said Lady Beatrice, maintaining eye contact until she felt his arm begin to tremble; at which point she turned and gazed out to sea. She gave a little sigh.

"Nobility and bravery are both called for, Miss Beatrice," said Mr. Pickett. "The specter of war may seem far off and unlikely to trouble us, but who can trust those French? And the Spaniard is just as bent on empire as he ever was, however feeble and impotent he may appear. And don't you think for a minute that those rebels in the former colonies wouldn't just jump at the chance to get square with us for beating them in the War of 1812." He glared angrily out to sea, as though to pierce the distance to America, quite unaware that he was gazing in the general direction of France. "Uncouth villains!"

Lady Beatrice, seeing the light of fanaticism beginning to blaze in his eyes once more, decided it was time to drag his attention back to the matter at hand. Observing the angle of the sunset, she turned in such a way as to allow the streaming golden light to display her charms to their greatest advantage. With wide eyes and parted lips, she gazed upon Mr. Pickett as though he were the hero of her dreams. It had its due effect on Mr. Pickett, who gulped, lurched forward under the irresistible influence of her beauty, and bent her backward in a kiss.

The embrace went on for some time, so it was fortunate that the garden was, as mentioned before, quite a private one. The object of Mr. Pickett's attentions neither screamed, struggled nor made any creditable attempt to resist him, and it was only his own sense of propriety which called a halt to the proceedings.

"Why—why, my dear Miss Beatrice, what must you think of me?" he said, gasping for breath. "I do humbly beg your pardon! I'll go down on my knees if you but ask. Only spare a poor mortal overcome by your radiant beauty!"

Lady Beatrice favored him with an expression that managed to convey the trepidation of a wounded fawn mixed with passionate adoration. She had learned to avoid the instinctive movements of quickly smoothing her garments, rearranging her décolletage, and tucking her hair back into place; a single forlornly dangling tress had the power to break hearts when properly presented. "Oh, Mr.

Pickett—dear Mr. Pickett—how can I tell you what I feel? But we must speak of this occurrence no further!" She raised her hands to her face, as in dismay. "And only think! Poor Mamma sleeps within."

Rueful (but not absolutely mortified), Mr. Pickett took Lady Beatrice's arm and was gratified when she clung to him. "I will be your perfect knight, Miss Beatrice. Pray, let me escort you to the good lady."

*A*s THEY MADE their way up the lodging house stairs, Lady Beatrice smoothed back her hair at last.

"Well, I've certainly won an admirer," she said, a trifle wearily. "I trust our absence proved useful?"

"It did that," said Mrs. Corvey. "Very interesting desk that man had, and I think the Gentlemen will want the matter pursued. I may have found a new cook, as well," she added thoughtfully.

"Splendid!"

"Well, it'll want some careful managing; wait and see. But we'll see what flattery and a higher wage can do."

"A little unscrupulous, is it not?"

"It's a hard business we're in, my dear."

They opened the door to their rooms to find Mrs. Otley seated at the table admiring something by lamplight, with the other ladies crowded around her.

"—but it looks so very grisly," Jane was complaining. "I really wish you had given it a proper burial."

"What's all this?" Mrs. Corvey set her cane in the umbrella stand and approached the table.

By way of response, Mrs. Otley turned the object that lay before her on the table and revealed it to be a skull.

"Erato found someone's head in Kents Cavern," said Herbertina.

"It's a *skull*," said Mrs. Otley with some heat. "And I'm not at all sure it belonged to a person. It looks very primitive to me."

The others made room at the table and Mrs. Corvey and Lady Beatrice sat down to consider Mrs. Otley's find. As skulls went (and Lady Beatrice had seen a few), it was certainly odd-looking. The skull was large, the teeth were remarkably long and the zygomatic bones were very broad. Although the cranial vault was high and wide, suggesting a large brain, there was evidence of a faint sagittal crest.

Mrs. Otley pointed at this last item and said defensively, "I'm quite sure that this is an archaic feature."

"Perhaps you found a Druid's head," suggested Miss Rendlesham.

"What a horrid thought!" said Maude.

"Not to one of a scientific mind," retorted Mrs. Otley. "I shall make a drawing of it and send it to Mr. Darwin. There was what appeared to be a grave or a midden there— I am quite sure I can unearth further specimens if I return. Perhaps it will turn out to be a find of great importance!"

"No doubt, my dear," said Mrs. Corvey, optics whirring as she examined the skull through different lenses. "Perhaps we won't keep it on the table where we take our tea, all the same, eh? Charlotte, I believe you have a hat box you can lend Erato?"

With a martyred air Miss Rendlesham fetched forth the box that had contained her ill-fated bonnet, and the skull was placed within. Such was its size, however, that the lid failed to quite close, giving the impression that the ghastly spectre of Death was peeping out through hollow eyes. This effect was slightly diminished by the pink ribbon they were obliged to tie around the box to keep the lid fastened.

As Mrs. Otley bore her trophy away to a side table, Herbertina said, "Oh! And you've another letter from the Gentlemen, Mrs. Corvey." She produced it from her jacket pocket and handed it across.

Mrs. Corvey took it with a sigh. "Well, there's half a night's work with the encryption book for me, and no mistake."

"May I help?" asked Lady Beatrice.

"I should be grateful," said Mrs. Corvey.

$\mathcal{L}$ADY BEATRICE LAID aside the encryption book. "I suppose, then, I shall be obliged to continue my romance with Mr. Pickett."

"Best way to find out what's what, isn't it?" said Mrs. Corvey, reaching for another sheet of foolscap. "Order No. 1: determine whether any further evidence of underwater craft exists. Answer: if the evidence of *my* eyes ain't enough, we can send a couple of the girls up on the cliffs at Daddyhole with a Talbotype camera.

"Order No. 2: determine probable location of docking for same. Answer: that'll be a nice trick, won't it? Though I expect he's using those sea caves under the cliff."

"I suppose I could try and wheedle it out of Mr. Pickett," said Lady Beatrice. "Assuming, of course, that he is in fact the culprit."

"He's bloody well up to *something*," said Mrs. Corvey, "from what I found on his desk. What's a gentleman want with all them incendiary devices, I should like to know? To say nothing of needing to pay for a cove with a forge? Which brings us to Order No. 3: determine evidence of manufactury. Answer: It looks obvious to me, but I expect a bit more digging through his desk is called for."

She looked at Lady Beatrice and raised an eyebrow. "Hope you don't find him too displeasing, my dear. You may be obliged to allow him a number of liberties."

Lady Beatrice made a dismissive gesture. "I make a firm distinction between duty and pleasure, Mrs. Corvey."

"That's the spirit, dear. Do make another discreet assignation, would you? With your dear mamma in attendance, of course. I should like another crack at that cook, as well." Mrs. Corvey settled down to draft her lengthy report to the Gentlemen. "Now, why don't you go take a little supper? See if you can't get some tea and toast sent up to me; I expect I won't get to bed before midnight."

HERBERTINA WAS ASSIGNED the role of amateur photographer, being judged the least likely to be remarked upon while wandering the cliff tops with a knapsack and a tripod. Nothing loathe, she traded her tailored day clothes for a loose coat and a cheerfully striped country neckerchief, donned a broad-brimmed straw against the sun, and marched off manfully to Daddyhole.

The path up the limestone cliffs was easy and gradual, but the day was very warm; before long, Herbertina's coat was hanging off the tripod strapped across her knapsack and her neckerchief hung loose. Her loose shirt and custom corsetry ensured that, even coatless, she displayed only the fashionable full chest of a well-dressed young man, and no revealing curves. And she was profoundly grateful, in the warmth of the day, that she could remove a layer of clothing and walk freely.

The cliff tops, when attained, were mostly unwooded, and she made her way through knee high herbage that sent up a smell like incense under the sun. The sea was a polished blue as calm as a ballroom floor, stretching away to what Herbertina fondly imagined was the seething coast of France (which had replaced its latest King with yet another Republic in February) but thought was probably a more mundane storm cloud far off in the Channel.

From time to time she stopped to set up the tripod and take the view, though she was saving the actual treated paper for the cottages that Mrs. Corvey had glimpsed from Mr. Pickett's carriage. The Gentlemen had made improvements to the Talbotype device that allowed the operator to load 14 ready-made blanks into the camera prior to use. However, changing the pack of light-sensitive paper was the part that Herbertina found most difficult to achieve without exposing all of them, so for now she contented herself with practice on the focusing lens and eyepiece adjustment.

Still, it was very pleasant to stroll along and play the naturalist, all alone in the shining summer morning. While not naturally a solitary person, as Lady Beatrice or Mrs. Otley were, Herbertina found it occasionally a great relief to be alone. It was easier to maintain privacy in one's own head during work (when, indeed, she was usually immersed in artistic personae) than it was in the girls' school atmosphere of the Ladies' private residence. She genuinely enjoyed the masculine quiet of clubs and bars, and so was now quite relishing her meander along the cliffs. The rolling emptiness of the cliff tops stretched all around her, and when she turned back from time to time, the white walls of Torbay looked like a wreath of lilies thrown down on the ruddy sands.

It was a little shy of midday when the rolling irregularity of the brush resolved itself into three tiny cottages. Herbertina set course for their chimneys, torn between hoping no one was home to ask her what she was doing and wondering if any of them had a working pump or well for an over-heated wanderer. To her pleasure, when she reached her goal she found both lack of inhabitants and an accessible well.

The cottages stood in a rough arc around the well, all facing the bay. They showed signs of recent repair, but were empty: no one came to the doors at Herbertina's hail, nor while she sloughed her hat and burdens and hauled up the well-bucket. When she was refreshed, she went and peered in each tiny front-facing window: neither furniture nor cottagers in the front rooms, though each showed a doorway into a windowless back room. Examining the back walls, it was obvious that there had once been windows: they were now bricked neatly up, hiding whatever was within. The doors, front and rear, were locked, which was a curious affectation in an isolated country cottage.

Pondering that, she took her first Talbotypes of the new brickwork, to document the anomaly. Then she returned and set up her tripod and camera in the shade of the wellhouse roof to wait for the anomalies for which she had actually come hunting.

$\mathcal{W}$ITH HERBERTINA OFF on her reconnaissance mission, Mrs. Otley also elected to take advantage of the fine weather and return to Kent's Cavern. None of the other Ladies were inclined to come with her, but that was not distressing—she quite enjoyed excavating on her own and understood that the joys of such physically active scholarship were not to every one's liking.

Indeed, very few women were so inclined. Until last year, Mrs. Otley had enjoyed a very satisfying correspondence with Mary Anning, who had made such remarkable discoveries in Lyme Regis on the Dorset coast. Of course, dear Mary had specialized in marine reptiles, and so would probably not have been that taken with the strange skull from Kents Cavern. It would have been pleasant, however, to discuss the dig itself with someone else conversant in the tricks and trials of excavation...alas, Mary Anning had succumbed to a cancer in her breast last year.

"'Grant unto them, we beseech Thee, Thy mercy and everlasting peace,'" murmured Mrs. Otley as she marched along, and somewhat self-consciously dedicated her day's digging in Mary's name. She had been raised in a High Church tradition, and the doing of good works was always a virtue.

It was barely two miles to Kent's Cavern, through an easily traversed wooded area; it was a little steep in places, but Mrs. Otley wore very sensible boots. The cave entrance was easily found amid the trees; indeed, it seemed to Mrs. Otley to be the very standard of a potential prehistoric dwelling. She thought she would have found it a suitable location herself, some thousands of years earlier.

She lit her little lantern and trudged on in. The constant cool temperature of the cave was a genuine pleasure on such a warm day; indeed, she could think of few day's work that would have been so pleasant in the sun as was a day's digging in a well-ventilated cavern.

The floors within were lightly sanded, and scattered with time-darkened stones fallen from the walls and ceilings. For the most part, the caverns were flowstone in a pleasing palette of salmon, grey and slatey blue—many portions were rich with both stalagmites and stalactites, and she proceeded with care so as to avoid crushing smaller and more fragile growths underfoot.

As she headed toward the meandering side chamber where she had found the fascinating skull, Mrs. Otley paused to study again an especially moving vista. She wondered whether primitive Britons could have deliberately carved what she now observed: a great face formed in the very substance of the walls. The middle part of the face was obliterated—possibly by the flowstone itself—but the lower portion showed a wide mouth, a quite strong chin and the base of what she fancied was a noble nose. With its broad cheekbones and high brow, she felt it had a definite resemblance to the skull she had found.

Treading carefully, she made her way to the slightly mounded area where the skull had been resting—it had been peering out at her with its dark empty sockets, as if standing guard in place of the great eyeless face in the distance. The scuff marks of her previous excavation now marked the place as clearly as a flag; she settled down in a nearly prayerful attitude, gave a slow contented sigh, and began to carefully remove small trowelfuls of the silky red dirt before her.

*T*HERE WAS NO wind; the sea lay flat under the heat and no boats marred its surface. Herbertina managed a Talbotype of a hovering hawk that perused her in turn from the middle air beyond the cliff edge, but rather felt that—aside from the neat trick of capturing the bird on the wing—the image had no real value. Still, it let her practice with the device. But when she did finally notice the wake on the ocean below, she was quite taken by surprise.

It showed up on the flat surface like a stroke of ink. There was no evident cause: there was still no wind, and there was no craft in sight, only an arrow-straight wake through the low glassy swell. Herbertina focused, pressed the activation lever, and re-focused as fast as she could. The wake was proceeding at a notable speed, seemingly creating itself from its own bow-wave, and Herbertina was twisting the lens and hauling on the lever with both frenzied hands, face pressed to the eyepieces.

Suddenly the leading edge of the wake opened up like a fountain. What emerged was not a jet of water, however, but a tall slender mast. Just behind it was something that looked like a leaning organ pipe, tilting past the mast. A massive shadow just below it suggested that some sizable body bore both objects aloft. Herbertina captured two successive images before the thing slid out of her field of vision. She straightened and frantically tried to loosen the horizontal holding screws—before she could, the mast once more submerged into its own wake. She could see it over the camera and tripod, even though she could not focus the device on it, and watched in astonishment as the wake, too, smoothed out and disappeared.

Either the thing had dissolved, or it had gone too deep to leave a wake. Herbertina cursed and stepped back from the tripod in surrender. She cursed still more when she discovered she had wound her neckerchief into the holding set screws, and was suddenly wearing the camera like a huge pendant. It cost her several minutes and the last two inches of her neckerchief to get free, kneeling on the ground bent over her mechanical albatross.

*M*RS. OTLEY WAS almost unaware of the passage of hours as she worked. The unchanging temperature and light in a cave were no indication of time; the constant small noises—a drip of distant water, the slide and whisper of a falling stone—did not occur in any living rhythm. However, the small watch she wore pinned to her bosom chimed the hour faithfully, and at last she had to regretfully admit she had excavated the better half of the day away.

And her lamp only held so much fuel. There were rumors of amazing devices available to field agents, lamps that ran on strange and sophisticated substances or gave one the night sight that Mrs. Corvey enjoyed. Mrs. Otley, however, was still a captive of whale oil.

As she sifted through a last spadeful of dirt, her reward suddenly tumbled into her hand like winning dice. Very like dice—they were, unless she much missed her guess, verte-bra—seven or eight of them, and very human-looking. Her excitement was great, but there was no time left to examine them closely. She drew a rough rectangle in the excavated dirt to mark where she had found them, then wrapped her trove carefully in a handkerchief and stowed it in her basket.

She fairly danced out of the cave, then, and blew a kiss to the great blind face as she passed it.

*M*RS. CORVEY STUDIED the fourteen Talbotypes on the table before her, anchored with perfume bottles, tea cups and two of the vases of flowers that had been arriving daily from Mr. Pickett (via the villainous Felan). She passed them one by one as she finished to Lady Beatrice and Mrs. Otley (just returned, rosy-cheeked and excited from her digging, and pressed immediately into service as an analyst). Those two ladies were the best suited to see details and patterns in the images, and possessed besides between them a good working knowledge of both marine life forms and ordnance.

"To dismiss the obvious at once," Mrs. Otley said, "this is not a whale. I think it is nothing alive at all."

"So much for the fishermen seeing Leviathans here-abouts," said Mrs. Corvey. "Something big's supposed to have come under one man's boat, though, and fetched it a good enough whack to pitch him overboard, and that looks big enough."

Her lenses made a soft whirring sound as she adjusted their light sensitivity, bringing one picture closer to her face. "That's *something*, for certain, just under the water—the light falls on it differently. What I can make out through the foam and glare looks like...a barge. A sunken barge. A barge underwater, at any rate. What on earth moves it?"

"There have been some very nearly successful attempts at submarine propulsion using steam engines. And treadmills, too. But they are very slow, I am told," offered Mrs. Otley.

"That thing isn't slow." Herbertina's voice was rather muffled. She lay on the sofa with her face on her folded arms, while Dora massaged neck muscles strained by the sudden weight of the Talbotype camera. "It went like bloody blazes! I barely had time to refocus and never did manage to change the paper pack—I'd have gotten more if I had. Sorry, Mrs. C."

"Not your fault, dear. You weren't anticipating a speed trial of the thing. Speaking of which, Erato, I don't think that a "very nearly successful" method can be what's driving this. A treadmill is a ponderous slow machine, I can tell you from my workhouse days."

"I don't see how a steam engine would work at all," said Miss Rendlesham from the window seat.

"It didn't," said Mrs. Otley in some embarrassment. "It blew up. I believe there was a problem with venting."

Lady Beatrice looked up from the image she was going over with a magnifying glass.

"Mrs. Corvey? Would you examine this, please? If you would, pay attention to that object that resembles an organ pipe."

Mrs. Otley took the image; her lenses whirred and extended slightly. After a moment, she asked incredulously, "Is that thing *smoking*? It is!"

"Yes, I thought so. Either they have solved the problem of submarine venting," said Lady Beatrice, "or that is a cannon."

The print was passed round with the magnifying glass, and the consensus was that it was, indeed, venting steam rather than the smoke of a spent charge. In verification, the next two prints in the series showed no impact in the water, which was as smooth ahead of the wake as behind it.

But Mrs. Otley, who had been perusing the print of the hawk proffered for her amusement by Herbertina, had spied something else in the background. On the cliffs beyond the cottages, below the imposing pile of Mr. Pickett's present domicile, was a figure. It was also watching the sea, and under examination by the magnifying glass appeared to be employing a telescope for the purpose. When Mrs. Corvey's lenses were brought to bear on the image, it was unmistakeably Mr. Pickett himself, watching the sea caves below the cottages and Herbertina's redoubt.

"I don't know what's being done, nor how he's doing it," said Mrs. Corvey in grim triumph, "but he's the bugger who's doing whatever it is! All right, the Gentlemen have put this off too long. I'm done with sending coy little love notes, it's time to break out the Aetheric Transmitter. I want to talk to someone about this, and I want to do it tonight!"

Dora and Maude trotted off at once to bring out Mrs. Corvey's sewing basket, and to reassemble its components into a compact Aetheric Transmitter; Miss Rendlesham obligingly ran the fine wire antenna out the window by which she had been sitting. Lady Beatrice meanwhile fetched out Mrs. Corvey's instruction manual and code books, and set about tuning the device to the frequency required by the date and hour for successful transmission. So accustomed were the Ladies to this exercise (by dint of regular drills with the equipment) that within a quarter hour Mrs. Corvey was determinedly demanding parlay with the Officer of the Day below Redking's Club in London, nearly 200 miles away.

Upon establishing bona fides to the disembodied male voice's satisfaction ("Who else does he think is calling out of the aether, I'd like to know?" muttered Mrs. Corvey *sotto voce* to the ladies seated expectantly round the table) it was at last determined that there was, essentially, no one of rank available for a serious consultation with field agents—let alone the holidaying Ladies of Nell Gwynne's.

"Then fetch Mr. Felmouth, young man," snapped Mrs. Corvey.

"Mr. Felmouth is the Head of Fabrication, ma'am," said the voice. It sounded somewhat scandalized.

"I know that, boy! You'll find him in the Artificer's Hall, I shouldn't wonder. The man's there all hours of the night and day." Mrs. Corvey pointed a finger at the Aetheric Transmitter, as if the man at the other end of the circuit were not as blind—or blinder—than she herself. "Something mighty odd is swanning round the coast off Torbay, and if all the Gentleman are off to Bath for the waters or whatever, then I'll have the Chief Fabricator to account. Put down that bun and go fetch him, now."

There was a most speaking silence, before the voice—now sounding positively unnerved—muttered "Yes'm," and the carrier wave was left to hum by itself.

"How did you guess he was eating a bun?" asked Maude, grinning.

"It's tea time," said Mrs. Corvey shortly.

"And if all the chiefs are off and out," commented Herbertina, "that boy was bound to have a cup or a pint or a bun to hand. Probably all three. Well done, Mrs. C."

Guilt or panic must have lent wings to the young operator's heels, because it was only a few minutes before Mr. Felmouth's familiar tones replaced the soft noise of the somnolent Transmitter.

"Felmouth here. How are you, Mrs. Corvey?" came his amused voice. "Young Harvey here is convinced your new lenses can now see along the beam of the Aetheric Transmitter. It's almost a pity to have to tell him I didn't make them *that* well. Though perhaps I'll let him think we are watching him, and so prevent crumbs from dropping into the Transmitter."

"Boys'll be boys. No matter how big they are," said Mrs. Corvey. "And most of the Gentlemen have taken French Leave, it seems. But we have something far too large and odd going on here for my girls to handle—especially on holiday!—and I need advice and decisions. Pardon my bluntness, Mr. Felmouth, but have you made a submarine boat for the Gentlemen?"

"What a...novel inquiry, Mrs. Corvey. Hmmm, hmmm. Ah, let me say: not *yet*," came his cautious reply.

"Someone has beat you to it, then. We have eye-witnesses—including *my* eyes, Mr. Felmouth, and you know what they can do, none better. My girls have seen the thing, and even on holiday they see what's there," said Mrs. Corvey. "Now, listen:

we have a dozen or so Talbotype prints, too, and they show that it's underwater, under power—probably steam—and possibly armed with a cannon. And if it's not the Gentlemen, then we have the culprit as well, and he's not a lad what I would trust with a borrowed dinghy, let alone a submarine boat! He's an American named Pickett, half-cocked at the best of times, and he's stock-piling munitions and has hired a foundryman and taken a house commanding the cliffs. Now I want someone to do something about this!"

"Good heavens," said Mr. Felmouth. "Surely you've reported this—this developing situation?"

"Repeatedly. And I've been told to watch and report, what I have done, and you can find the reports on file somewhere under Harvey's tea mug, I've no doubt. What I need now is someone to come take over before Mr. Pickett declares war on France. The man is mad to defend the Queen, and he'll invent an enemy if he has to." Mrs. Corvey gave a sharp nod at the Transmitter, then said in closing, "Can you be of assistance, Mr. Felmouth?"

"I hardly know. The Field branch is—well, they are all in the field, you see, and I know it's quite a scramble over there at the moment, which is probably why they did not act with alacrity on a, a domestic situation…" Mr. Felmouth's distracted voice trailed off a moment, then resumed with new firmness. "But I certainly know upon whom to call, and how to hurry this through channels, Mrs. Corvey, and please rest assured I will! Can you leave the Transmitter up, with someone monitoring it for my reply? I shall have an answer for you this evening."

Miss Rendlesham, still in the window seat reading her novel, raised a hand to volunteer. Mrs. Corvey and Mr.

Felmouth closed with mutual courtesies and some haste, and Lady Beatrice set the Transmitter to its holding setting.

"And now," announced Dora brightly, "it's time for *our* tea! Imagining that poor boy clutching his bun all alone, so far away..."

"Oh, don't," said Maude. "I don't want to think of poor boys clutching anything! We're on holiday."

"Such as it is," said Mrs. Corvey. "Well, girls, two or three of you go down and fetch us up with a good solid tea. We'll eat *en suite* while we wait to find out what else we have to do. I fancy something toasted today, I think."

*J*ARDINES ON TOAST went far to restore Mrs. Corvey to her usual calm; her lenses stopped their nervous whirring in and out, which was always a sure sign she was in a temper. A plate of local mushrooms and cheese thrilled Mrs. Otley, and the others were happily confronted with an array of muffins, cold meats and warm breads. Three kinds of tea and copious cream reduced Dora, Jane and Maude to a cat-like somnolence, and even the other Ladies to a quiet content.

But Miss Rendlesham, now reclining at her ease on the chaise beside the end table that housed the Transmitter, was immediately ready when it chimed three times to announce an incoming message. Teacup neatly held in thumb and forefinger, she hit the Receive button with her ring finger while pushing up the volume lever with the edge of the novel in her other hand. She was sitting up and announcing, "Mrs. Corvey is to hand and ready for transmission," as soon as Mr. Felmouth's voice gave tentative greeting.

Mrs. Corvey was just finishing a pot of Earl Grey tea (she had been pleased to find the exotic blend, widely available only for the last ten years or so, on their boarding house's menu) and thus inquired quite amiably after Mr. Felmouth's news. He, however, sounded less than equable in his address.

"To tell you the honest truth, Mrs. Corvey," he said across the miles, "we simply have no qualified men to send out there at this time. There is no one left in Field save for a few trainees."

"Where on earth are they, Mr. Felmouth?" said Mrs. Corvey.

"Well, they are—they are all out, ah—managing revolutions. As it were. So to speak." Mr. Felmouth was obviously both taken aback at the admission, and chastened to report his failure. "It appears that not only is the recent French trouble still fermenting, but several other European powers, both major and minor, are building up to similar explosions, and our best operatives are all abroad making sure it all ends— ah, ends well."

"Are the Gentlemen for or against this tide of revolution?" inquired Mrs. Corvey with marked restraint. "Oh, never mind—hardly matters to us here, does it?

"Well, have you any advice at all for what we shall do here in the civilized backwaters with our mad American submariner?"

"I am instructed to advise you that, regretfully, the matter must be placed fully in your hands for the next few days," said Mr. Felmouth. "You are to watch this Pickett fellow closely, gathering such proof of his activities as may be managed, and stand ready to stop him if the need arises suddenly. There should be operatives free to take over from you by the end of next week, if the matter has not come to a head before then."

"And presumably to keep my girl out of gaol, when she's had to stab the bugger to keep him from playing Drake with the French shipping?" asked Mrs. Corvey. She raised an admonitory hand as Mrs. Otley gave a little cry. "Did you *read* my reports? We didn't pack for field duty ourselves, you know. Beatrice will probably have to dispatch Mr. Pickett with a knitting needle, if it comes to it."

"Oh...oh, surely not," said Mr. Felmouth faintly. "Surely it is not so serious as that? Your reports were alarming, true, but surely it will not come to violence?"

Lady Beatrice leaned toward the Transmitter, asking Mrs. Corvey's permission with a raised eyebrow. "Mr. Felmouth, Lady Beatrice here. I have had a more intimate view of Pickett's ambitions, and he really is quite out of control. He dreams of imperial favor and a hero's career. He seems to have built a vessel that will travel underwater, and he is certainly manufacturing munitions. He has employed a foundry. In fact, it appears he has constructed a submarine gun platform. I am not, of course, *au courant* with our government policies regarding the French, but I should think that opening fire on their ships will have an adverse effect on our relations with their new Republic? There were riots and massacres in Paris only last month."

The Transmitter hummed. A warble in the carrier wave grew into a low moaning sound, which was evidently originating with Mr. Felmouth.

"Mr. Felmouth. Do pay attention, Mr. Felmouth," said Mrs. Corvey sternly. "Pickett's got no grasp of real politics, and he's got nothing to stop him out here but an infatuation with our Beatrice. He's a romantic fool, but he's dangerous. We shall do the best we can to slow him, and stop him if we must—but you get us some help out here at once, you understand? Send us some of your new toys, maybe, until the Gentlemen can settle their revolutions and get here to tend to home business."

Mr. Felmouth's vocal distress cleared to a rush of apologies and promises of immediate help, "—of the best I can ready, Mrs. Corvey, at once and by special courier. I'll send out whatever I can without delay. And I'll see what I can do to get some of the Field lads back from Hungary, and Czechoslovakia, and the Piedmont: so many of them are in the Piedmont, you see, and then the Slavs are revolting—"

Jane and Dora stifled giggles in the sofa cushions.

"—but I'm sure the Austrian group can be pulled out, and of course they won't be needed in Rome until November..."

Mrs. Corvey interrupted gently: "Mr. Felmouth, I rather think we've heard quite enough. Just send us what you can, and we'll do our best with Mr. Pickett."

With garbled assurances and apologies, and a complete disregard of the usual protocols, Mr. Felmouth finally signed off; or, as it sounded, was forcibly signed off by Harvey. Jane and Dora finally burst out laughing over the revolting Slavs, and Mrs. Corvey leaned back in her chair, massaging her temples round the brass rims of her ocular implants.

"Yes, yes, get your jollies now, my girls. God only knows what we'll find ourselves doing before this all ends," she said.

"I wonder what he's sending?" mused Herbertina.

"Well, at least we're still on holiday, until Mr. Felmouth's toys arrive or Mr. Pickett goes a-pirating across the Channel," said Miss Rendlesham practically. "And the evening is still young. Who'd like a few hands of whist?"

$\mathcal{T}$HE MYSTERIES AND mischief of Treadway Pickett did not manage to rule their holiday time. There were the long, casual days to enjoy, the warm nights, and hours untrammeled by any vestige of professional duties. There was shopping, there were books, there were long walks—while Mrs. Otley had vigorous physical hobbies that took her outdoors, all the Ladies enjoyed the opportunity to simply go strolling in the sunlight. Herbertina and the Deveres were on the beach every day, so enthused with sea-bathing that Mrs. Corvey was obliged to warn them about spoiling their complexions.

On 14 July, a freight dray came laboring up the street to the boarding house where the Ladies of Nell Gwynne's were staying. Wagons full of cargo and luggage were not an unfamiliar sight in the streets of Torbay, of course; but they rarely had respectable ladies perched on the driver's seat. This one did, although she did not handle the reins herself, but sedately directed the driver (who resembled a tidily-dressed satyr) with her furled parasol. When they reached the boarding house, she dismounted and sent the dray on into the paved inner courtyard. She herself entered the building and sent the parlor maid to announce that Mrs. Sarah Goodman had arrived to meet with Master Herbert Corvey.

The maid found Master Herbert alone on the third-story smoking porch, cigar in hand, peering over the railing to where the drayman was unloading a coffin sized (and shaped) crate.

"What d'you suppose that is, Jenny?" Herbertina inquired casually as the maid curtsied.

"Don't know, sir, but the lady who came on the drayer's cart is in the front hall asking to see you. A Mrs. Sarah Goodman," replied Jenny a little stiffly.

She thought young Master Herbert very handsome, with a sweet mouth and lovely bronze curls; it was such a shame, about the cigars and hair pomade—and now older ladies come a-calling! She sniffed disapprovingly but waited for Master Herbert's response.

Herbertina had no idea who Mrs. Sarah Goodman was. However, behind Jenny Mrs. Corvey had appeared in their sitting room: her eyebrows arched in surprise above her smoked glasses, but she smiled and nodded at the name, signaling that it was well. She promptly vanished back into the rooms, but Herbertina was accustomed to improvising relationships on the fly.

"Ah, dear Aunt Goodman! Arrived on the luggage cart, did she?" Herbertina extinguished her cigar in the brass sand urn on the rail. "She's an original, is Auntie. Thank you, Jenny."

She pressed a farthing into Jenny's hand, then turned and strode down the stairs to the front parlor.

Mrs. Goodman was seated in the front parlor, just tucking her gloves into her bonnet. Herbertina hurried up and reached for her hands, exclaiming "Aunt Goodman! I say, what a surprise to see you here. Mamma said nothing of your visiting."

Mrs. Goodman smiled, a small cat-like smile. Indeed, her entire face—though round and rather plain at first glance—was enlivened with an air of felinity: a smiling triangular mouth, pointed little nose, and a general air of knowing amusement. Her eyes were a bright pale blue; her curly hair an unremarkable brown that showed hints (to Herbertina's professional eyes) of having being hennaed in the not-too-distant past. Her clothes were very good and very respectable, but did not altogether hide the fact that her form, too, had the easy voluptuousness of a relaxed tabby.

She let her hand lie properly unresisting in Herbertina's own for a moment before drawing it back. Patting Herbertina's smooth cheek, Mrs. Goodman motioned for her to join her on the couch.

"I was passing through on an errand for a *Gentleman* of our acquaintance," said Mrs. Goodman, with a sidelong look and slight emphasis, "and I thought how nice it would be to see dear Elizabeth. And since she had told me how you were suddenly shooting up into a proper young man, I thought I would deliver a little gift you might find amusing. I understand you are quite athletic?"

"I take a bit of sport, of course," agreed Herbert cautiously. Mrs. Goodman's general air of a cat at a mousehole made her uncertain as to which of her professions was being referenced.

"Yes, I thought so," said Mrs. Goodman. "Now, come into the yard with me, dear boy, and see what I have brought for you.

The drayman had levered the lid off the mysterious box when Mrs. Goodman and Herbertina came into the court-yard. Packing straw was scattered on the cobblestones. He saluted with a wave of pry bar to forelock, and gestured down into the box.

"Have it out in just a moment, mum. Sorry for the delay—it took a bit to get it free, it's that awkward."

With that, he dropped the pry and reached into the box with both arms. With obvious effort, he lifted out a vaguely pony-shaped thing, hauling it out with about the ease a man would exhibit trying to decant a real pony from a wooden box. He set it on the ground, leaning it against the box, where it stood stiffly tilted.

"There you are," said Mrs. Goodman. She beamed as if she had just presented Herbertina with her heart's desire. Herbertina stared.

The thing had two wheels—not sensibly side by side, as in a cart, but one in front of the other. They were wooden and spoked, with iron tires. The rear wheel was twice the size of the front one, and connected to it by a jointed linkage armature framing the front wheel. The front also bore two treadles on long rods, by which the armature was apparently moved. Between the two wheels was a long, curving body bearing a small saddle with a high back; at the front, over-hanging the wheel, it was carved into the semblance of a spirited horse's head. A crescent-shaped tiller handle framed the horse's neck, attached to the front wheel and clearly meant to be accessible to whomsoever was seated on the saddle. The entire contrivance gleamed in the sun, being made of polished oak and brass.

"Why, Aunt, it's...what is it, precisely?" asked Herbertina.

"It's a sort of dandy horse," said Mrs. Goodman. "There was quite a fad some time before you were born, just before the 1820s. The Germans called them Laufmaschines, and they were a sort of rolling hobby-horse: the riders straddled them and pushed along with their feet. They were so hard to steer, you know, and so fast—up to eight miles per hour, imagine!—that they were finally banned in most places. The riders kept running over people on the pavements. This particular machine has been much improved by a Scottish *Gentleman*"—again, the sidelong glance from under her lashes "—named

Kirkpatrick Macmillan. The addition of treadles and the linkage arm allow it to be propelled by the rider, and since the tiller handles turn the front wheel, it is much more easily steered!"

"I see," said Herbertina, who actually could not imagine the acrobatics required.

"Of course, one could not fall off the old hobby-horses very easily, whereas one must balance on this model, and stay upright by the use of momentum. Or so I am told," said Mrs. Goodman. She looked at Herbertina's legs critically. "You have a good length of limb, nephew, so I should think you can handle this quite well."

Herbertina stared helplessly at the dandy horse, and finally summoned up an inquiry: "Are there instructions?"

"No. Not really." Mrs. Goodman appeared to be suppressing a smile. "But I have seen the device in operation, and I will stay here for an hour or two and see how you get on. I am certain you will master it in no time, Herbert—you have ridden much more difficult mounts, I am sure!"

That may have been true, but Herbertina had ample time that afternoon to consider that her previous mounts, no matter how wild, had actually wanted to be ridden. The dandy horse was not so inclined.

The next hour or two gave Herbertina a great intimacy with the operation of the dandy horse. The greatest trick appeared to be the crucial moment when one lifted one's feet off the ground and onto the treadles, and then pedaled like a desperate sailor on the pumps of a sinking hulk. Unfortunately, this also gave her an increasing familiarity with the cobbled floor of the courtyard, especially as Mrs. Goodman's instructions ran heavily to: "Faster, faster! Now *steer*! Left, left—your *other* left! Oh, dear..."

Fortunately, the sounds of Mrs. Goodman's cries and Herbertina's curses, mingled with the drayman's laughter, soon fetched down Dora, Maude and Jane. They were both appalled and fascinated, and with their aid as a sort of living mounting frame, Herbertina began to make real progress in getting on and staying on long enough to propel the cunning machine forward. The next step was the actual steering—with Maude and Dora running alongside and hauling with her on the curving handle, Herbertina finally began to grasp how to coordinate the diverse acrobatics the machine demanded. Braking—which required removing one's feet from the treadles and dragging one's boot heels—proved must simpler than driving forward, at least once Herbertina stopped falling over when her momentum was absorbed.

At length, however, she rode triumphantly and alone round the yard, sole commander of her now-biddable dandy horse, whooping with delight. The Devere sisters jumped up and down and applauded wildly; and as Herbertina finally slowed to a perfect stop before Mrs. Goodman, yet more applause sounded from the third-floor balcony of the boarding house. The other Ladies stood there clapping their hands, and Miss Rendlesham threw down a rose, calling "Bravo! Bravo! Bravissimo!"

Mrs. Goodman declined the offer of lunch with Mrs. Corvey, as she had to catch an afternoon train back to some carefully unspecified destination. She did consent to a refreshing cup of tea and a quiet chat before she left; the Ladies, gathering that Mrs. Goodman was a successful alumna of Nell Gwynne's, left the two older women alone in their suite's sitting room. Mrs. Corvey was most uncharacteristically giggling with their visitor as the younger Ladies sought other occupation for a while.

Mrs. Otley took her calipers, measuring tape, lap desk and the bones from Kent's Cavern and retired to the bedchamber she shared with Miss Rendlesham to answer a letter from her correspondent, Mr. Darwin. (He had responded with some enthusiasm to her original description a few days previously.) Miss Rendlesham rather objecting to Mrs. Otley's hollow-eyed visitor, she took her ubiquitous book and joined everyone else in the inner courtyard to watch Herbertina practice on the dandy horse.

This provided considerable amusement for an hour or so, with Herbertina growing steadily more confident and daring on the machine. The Devere sisters were wild to try it themselves, and Dora lamented not bringing any of her schoolgirl costumes: but Lady Beatrice tactfully pointed out that they were hoping to avoid notice, which would be quite impossible if Dora were to proceed down Market Street or Babbacombe Road with her knees flashing free.

"I suppose that means we may not try it in our bathing costumes on the beach, either," sighed Maude. "I suppose it is best to keep it secret."

"In fact, we should probably go indoors with it now," said Lady Beatrice. "Our fellow lodgers have missed this demonstration, but they will be coming back for lunch now, I think. Time to put away Herbertina's fascinating toy."

"Especially as I suspect I'm meant to use this to go hunt sea caves full of submarine boats and floating cannons," put in Herbertina. "I thought I would try that tonight, you know. The moon is full; there should be plenty of light."

"You should rest, then," said Miss Rendlesham, closing her book and standing up. "And certainly change your clothes! Your trouser cuffs are destroyed, and you will surely want rougher clothes for tonight."

The drayman having departed with the box in which the dandy horse had come, they stashed it in the stables with their own trunks and covered it with a horse blanket. Miss Rendlesham carefully affixed the label from Mrs. Corvey's own trunk to the blanketed lump, which they adjudged should render it invisible to any of the staff until it was time to depart for home.

Mrs. Goodman had departed when they all trooped back upstairs, but she had left behind a box of further surprises for everyone else. Mrs. Corvey, in a rare expansive mood, passed out some odd-looking items: what were surely busks and corset stays, but made of a smooth black fibrous material.

"And these are also from Mr. Felmouth," she said, "for the rest of us. He must be sending us everything loose in the Fabrication Department! He writes to say he is not sure what use these may be, but he also advises that they are much lighter than ordinary stays and even stronger. An experimental effort at making artificial whalebone, I gather."

"Lighter stays are always a grand idea. And stronger ones, too; work does get rather vigorous at times..." said Miss Rendlesham. She rubbed a cautious finger along a busk, but the color remained fast. "What are they made of?"

"He claims they are made from a fiber somehow spun from pitch, and reinforced with glue," said Mrs. Corvey. "And as daft as *that* sounds, there's more: he says that if these are used in place of ordinary stays, they should prove proof against both knives and small arms fire!"

"Then they ought to be marvelous against badly aimed champagne corks, said Jane. "Which I do most sincerely hope will continue to be the worst thing we encounter."

"Well, I'll try them out tonight," said Herbertina gamely. "If they can stand up against the rigors of the dandy horse, they should be proof against playful MPs, don't you think?"

Lady Beatrice, having already fetched her second-best corset, looked up from where she was carefully unpicking a pertinent seam.

"I imagine tonight may well tell," she said gravely, and set her own corset aside. "To which end, Herbertina, do bring me one of your special corsets and I will make the changes for you before you go out this evening."

She looked at Mrs. Corvey, and added, "Along with his usual daily flowers, Mr. Pickett has invited us to a picnic supper this evening. I have accepted, so as to make sure that he, at least, is distracted. And should it require serious measures to keep him from the cliff tops, it would be better if there were nothing peculiar for him to find out about *my* corset. The man is an engineer, after all."

"If he can think about engineering after getting down to your corset, he's a match for us," said Herbertina gallantly. "Wear that one with the dozens of little bows, and he'll spend hours as busy as a kitten with a ball of yarn!"

$\mathcal{A}$s THE AFTERNOON went on, Lady Beatrice methodically replaced stays in one of Herbertina's custom corset (plain white duck, in the masculine style favored by gentlemen of youthful aspirations but spreading waistlines).

Mrs. Otley, having rejoined them all in the parlor, reported excitedly on Mr. Darwin's agreement with her that the Kents Cavern skull was quite peculiar. She was preparing another letter regarding the vertebrae she had also found. Miss Rendlesham made a few rather perfunctory remarks about the general dreadfulness of the project, but finally allowed that a quasi-human fossil was indeed more interesting than yet another sea monster; of which, she commented, they seemed to have a sufficiency.

The Devere sisters promised all and sundry that they would utilize Mr. Felmouth's gifts at the very earliest opportunity; they then promptly went off to the beach for a splash, accompanied by the patient Herbertina as escort.

"It's like running a nursery sometimes with that lot. Or keeping kittens," Mrs. Corvey said as they went chattering out. "But there—they're good girls in a pinch and do liven the place up. You just have to keep them from getting bored."

"I cannot imagine the Devere sisters bored," said Lady Beatrice dryly.

In such pleasant ordinary pastimes the hours went by. If one were unaware that Lady Beatrice was replacing corset stays with an eye to enhancing the armour capabilities of her fellow whore, or that Mrs. Otley was lecturing Miss Rendlesham about the possible discovery of a prediluvian sub-human, it would have seemed the very ideal of a domestic scene. When Mrs. Corvey decreed that tea would be taken downstairs with their fellow lodgers (in part to forestall questions from anyone who might have observed the dandy horse exercises), the fossils and armour stays were laid aside and they went down discussing the replacement of Miss Rendlesham's ill-fated seaside bonnet.

The bathers returned as tea was finishing up, and the family adjourned *en masse* upstairs once more, with Master Herbert teasingly speculating on the horrible crop of freckles his sisters were sure to have incurred in their afternoon excursion. Their progress was loudly hilarious all the way up the stairs, to the amusement of the other lodgers below.

"Right then," said Mrs. Corvey briskly as the door closed behind them and the cover conversation was abandoned. "Herbertina, you go have a lie down before this evening. The moon doesn't rise until quarter past nine or so, and you should be as rested as possible before you try that thing on the cliff path."

Herbertina saluted smartly and went off to the room she shared with the Deveres. The sisters busied themselves assembling a scratch meal of sandwiches and lemonade for themselves, and made up a packet for Herbertina to take with her on her next foray.

"That gandy horse needs a basket or saddlebags or something," commented Jane.

"*Dandy*, not gandy," corrected Maude. "It would be useful to secure a light to it somehow, too, for night use."

"Not tonight," said Mrs. Corvey. "Tonight, we want Herbertina to be as invisible as possible, and that full moon will light up her as well as the cottages. When you've finished that package, girls, see to it that she's got clothes laid out that ain't too bright *or* dark. Greys and browns, like; maybe that lavender coat of hers—it'll fade out nicely and slide by the eye in moonlight."

"People mostly see what they expect to see, after all," observed Lady Beatrice. She held up the finished corset, now securely lined with Mr. Felmouth's strange stays. "And no one will expect to see Herbertina up there tonight, which will help. If she dresses darkly and keeps to the shadows, she should be able to see and yet not be seen."

"We shall see. Or not. And that," said Mrs. Corvey, "is the point, ain't it?"

The lamps were lit in the parlor eventually. Beyond the front windows, the eastern sky over the Channel was showing the barest hint of a glow where the moon would rise soon. There was no fog off the bay tonight, only the deep blue summer twilight.

Lady Beatrice and Mrs. Corvey had left in Mr. Pickett's carriage an hour before, when there was still a bright sky and gold on the sea. Now Miss Rendlesham was setting up the Aetheric Transmitter, just in case one of their enterprises abroad in the night should call in. Both Herbertina and Lady Beatrice carried small devices that resembled pill boxes—called sparkers, when operated they emitted bursts of Aetheric energy that could be detected on the receiver as a series of pops and squeaks. There were a number of pre-arranged codes that all the Ladies had committed to memory, and the new American Morse Code more than sufficed for longer messages.

"I don't know if I hope you see something or not," said Mrs. Otley. "It all sounds so dangerous, and we are supposed to be on holiday!"

Herbertina was up and dressed, in more subdued colors than was her wont. She looked up from winding a spare scarf about one trouser leg, puttee-style, to prevent its being frayed by the dandy horse's treadles.

"Well, Erato, unexpected things are supposed to happen on holiday, aren't they?" she said cheerfully. "You discovered your funny skull, Charlotte was attacked by a seagull, and Mrs. C. has found a sea monster. Or a pirate. And I'll nail which it is tonight! Then we can all go back to hunting sea shells and wondering if there'll be lemon curd for tea."

So saying, she tipped her cloth cap at the room in general, and sauntered out the door. The Devere sisters went quietly out to the balcony to watch her progress to the stable and out of the dark courtyard. Though the Ladies still in the rooms listened intently, there was almost no noise from down below—a creak from the stable doors, a whirring noise, and then a soft metallic drone that must have been the iron tires on the cobbles.

"She was a bit wobbly on the corner," reported Dora, coming in. "But she straightened right up and went off down the street at a great speed! It looks like tremendous fun."

"More importantly, it looks like it will work. It's silent and nearly invisible in the dark," added Jane.

The sisters settled down to work on their corsets. Miss Rendlesham read aloud from the final chapter of *Dombey and Son,* while they all sat waiting for the Aetheric Transmitter to make some revelatory sound.

*I*N THE SAME silken blue twilight, Lady Beatrice and Mr. Pickett strolled along the cliff tops that fronted his rented villa.

They had picnicked pleasantly enough in the lee of his garden walls, Mrs. Corvey having pled an aversion to the sea wind on her face as she ate. However, as there was patently no wind at all this evening, that served to keep Mr. Pickett from the cliffs only for a brief duration; indeed, his eagerness to venture there alone with Lady Beatrice was so obvious as to be barely decent. When Mrs. Corvey had finally announced she would retire for a post-prandial rest, Mr. Pickett had helped her indoors with such alacrity her feet barely seemed to touch the ground.

He then rejoined Lady Beatrice. She noted with some amusement that he apparently would not have cared had he known that Mrs. Corvey was settling in to pillage his desk and suborn his cook, so anxious was he to get Beatrice to himself.

She was resigned to a certain athleticism in the course of the coming evening, which she felt sure would distract Mr. Pickett even if the growing moonlight were to reveal Herbertina actively scuttling whatever craft was hidden in the sea caves.

The path was meandering, but neatly cut into the soil and covered with a fine gravel that reflected the last light with soft clarity. Lady Beatrice, noting that the edges were sharp and clean, looked a little more closely and saw that it still retained parallel wheel marks: something quite heavy had been wheeled back and forth on this little pathway, something wider than a wheelbarrow but much narrower than any carriage or pony-cart. She doubted the tidy work on the path was attributable to the estate agents from whom Mr. Pickett had leased the house.

When the upper windows of the house were obscured by a turn round a rise of land, Lady Beatrice sighed and leaned subtly toward Mr. Pickett as they walked. Reflexively—as she expected—his arm rose and encircled her waist. The quickening pulses in his chest and fingers were just discernible through the satin of her bodice. She lay her hand on his where it rested against her side, and matched his stride with a little skip neatly obscured by her skirts; so that they settled, by her artifice, into an effortless and perfectly rhythmic pace together.

Lady Beatrice judged that Mr. Pickett was by now quite thoroughly distracted. She was therefore unsurprised when he suddenly stopped, and turned her firmly in his arms to face him.

"Miss Beatrice—lovely Beatrice, if I may be so bold—I must unburden myself to you," he said hoarsely. "I would not risk your good opinion or your safety for all the world—I'm sure you know that—but...my darling Beatrice, may I tell you a great secret?"

Lady Beatrice had become accustomed to feigning enthusiasm at all manner of requests—but at this fevered query, she smiled up at Mr. Pickett in genuine delight. To judge by his dilating pupils, the effect was devastating.

"Dearest Tredway," she murmured, gazing up with sincere pleasure lighting her grey eyes, "you may tell me *anything.*"

*M*RS. CORVEY HAD made herself as comfortable as possible in Mr. Pickett's austere sitting room. She had a brief but profitable rifle through his desk—still unlocked; the man had utterly unwarranted trust in the servants he treated so cavalierly—and even went so far as to slip a few receipts into her reticule. There were alarming numbers of them from his foundry connections, which provided potentially useful tidbits such as names, locations and quantities of work. It appeared his project was approaching completion.

There were also several pages of good stationery, filled with much-crossed-out and amended declarations of his love for Lady Beatrice. Mrs. Corvey was amused to see he was evidently on the verge of proposing marriage, but was having trouble working up either his nerve or the appropriate wording. She wouldn't have thought the brash and self-aggrandizing Mr. Pickett was so shy...on the other hand, maybe he was struggling to find a way to phrase his plans for international piracy in a manner that would please a mother-in-law.

Considering the image of Pickett in his scarlet highwayman's coat, down on one knee to ask her for Lady Beatrice's hand, diverted Mrs. Corvey considerably as she composed herself once more on the settee. She rang for the parlor maid, and requested that Mrs. Drumm please attend her with some of her excellent pastries and a fresh pot of tea.

Footsteps sounded outside the parlor door in a gratifyingly brief time. Mrs. Corvey considered that Mrs. Drumm must have been keeping an eye out for her master's guests and been prepared; which evidence of professional skill was very heartening. She was also pleased to see that the cook arrived alone with the refreshments, and entered with a nice little cough to announce herself to the "blind" Mrs. Corvey.

"Oh, Mrs. Drumm, is it you?" inquired Mrs. Corvey unnecessarily.

"Indeed, madam, as you requested." Mrs. Drumm set down the tray, which was properly set with only a single teacup. From the pocket of her apron, though, she drew a second teacup which had been discreetly stashed so that the intimate nature of their meeting was not blatantly advertised.

She pulled up a chair and then poured for them both, plated a nice pair of lemon tarts, and leaned forward to guide one plate and fork into Mrs. Corvey's hands.

"There you are, madam," she said. "And I hopes all is to your satisfaction?"

"You are a wonder of efficiency, Mrs. Drumm," said Mrs. Corvey. She took a bite of her tart, and would have rolled her eyes had she still had them. "And an artist in the kitchen…I trust you received my note of two days past?"

Mrs. Drumm cut out a forkful of her own tart with martial precision and a grim smile, looking rather like a domestic Boudicca with her red hair coiling round her head in little flame-like points.

"I did that, madam," she confirmed. "And very welcome it was, too. If I get one more scolding on how to joint birds or make porridge out of maize—Maize! We feeds it to the pigs where I was raised!—I'm like to run mad, I tell you."

Mrs. Corvey made a sympathetic moue. "I quite understand. Now, your half-holiday is Saturday, as I recall. Well, Mrs. Drumm, I do believe we may suit one another very well, but I'd never want to be less than open with an artiste like yourself. One always wants to make quite, quite sure that a new person will fit comfortably into the household, you know. Especially when there are delicate situations—" she made a vague embarrassed gesture at her black glasses "—to be considered. So, how should you feel about coming to my lodgings for some discussion tomorrow? I should like you to meet my family. All my girls."

"Very liberal and fine of you, Mrs. Corvey," said Mrs. Drumm. "A household of good decent Englishwomen would be a blessing, I am not ashamed to say!"

"Well, there is also my son Herbert," interposed Mrs. Corvey. Mrs. Drumm waved a hand, conceding the point, but continued:

"Well, yes, but your Master Herbert's an Englishman, ain't he?"

"Oh, yes." Mrs. Corvey savored another bite of tart. "Herbert is most certainly—English."

$\mathscr{O}$UT ON THE cliff road, Herbertina was proceeding along in the growing moonlight with confident glee. She'd had to walk the dandy horse up the steeper bits of the path when it proved unequal to being driven up the slopes; nonetheless, it was a faster, smoother progress than walking. There was an undeniable exhilaration in the movement of the treadles— like seven league boots, they took the ordinary motion of the legs and sped the rider on in enormous strides. Downhill slopes were an absolute delight, a delicious rush through the night air at what felt like tremendous speed! And the vibration transmitted up through the chassis to the saddle was... interesting, as well.

She hoped Mr. Felmouth wouldn't want it back.

She topped a gentle rise about a half-mile from the cottages, and braked to an abrupt stop. The cottages were a blaze of light, yellow flickering lamplight as well as the steadier glow of gas jets. Judging from the copious illumination that spilled from the doorways, gas lines had been laid on generously in all three buildings.

The yard defined by the arc of cottages bustled with activity. Men moved purposefully everywhere. The well itself was a focus of movement, and even at Herbertina's distance it was obviously standing taller now than the cottage roofs.

"An unexpected erection. How surprising," said Herbertina aloud, and giggled. She pushed off again and coasted silently down the slope in the darkness.

APPROXIMATELY HALF A mile on the other side of the cottages, Mr. Pickett and Lady Beatrice reclined against a convenient berm grown with fragrant thyme. At least Mr. Pickett rhapsodized about its being thyme; Lady Beatrice thought it more a mix of chamomile and miner's lettuce, but was too polite and too professional to correct her escort's claims to any expertise. In any event, it was both soft and aromatic, which was enough for Lady Beatrice. It did not distract her as she lay in Pickett's arms, listening attentively.

He had recapped for her his devotion to England, and his late-in-life decision to apply his energy and skills to the benefit of the Mother Country. He stressed again his admiration for the gentlemen adventurers of the gloried past; he bemoaned the passivity of the current generation on both sides of the Atlantic. He assured Lady Beatrice of his determination to put his aspirations into concrete form and physical action.

As he orated thus, Lady Beatrice was aware of the increasing tension in his arms about her. Mr. Pickett did not seem to notice this, nor the matching excitement that manifested itself against Lady Beatrice's thigh even through the folds of her skirts. Mr. Pickett's *body* was much more aware, apparently, than his busy mind; and Lady Beatrice writhed slowly and subtly in his embrace so as to encourage its attention.

"I am a man of action," Mr. Pickett assured Lady Beatrice. "I aim to prove myself to England as a knight aspirant to his lady. Real deeds, that's the measure of a man!"

Lady Beatrice was silent, gazing upward with wordless and admiring inquiry.

"Dearest Beatrice...I know I can confide in you," Pickett said rather hoarsely. "You know I am a sailor, and an engineer. For England's honor and glory, I have built an entirely new kind of ship—indeed, a new kind of weapon! And it will all be for England's good! My bridal gift to the country I mean to, to...espouse, you...might say..."

"*Yes,*" was all Lady Beatrice did say as he paused. However, Mr. Pickett's body finally took control of the conversation in this lull, and as she looked upward through lowered lashes, he at last fell silent for a moment and pressed his mouth violently to hers.

Even through frenzied kisses, however, he related the details of his devoted artificery. Lady Beatrice need do no more than return his kisses—with a carefully calculated rate of rising ardor, timed against her own heartbeat—and occasionally murmur "Yes?" in an interrogative tone.

"—it operates by steam power, you see. Silent, inexorable, irresistible steam power," he mumbled against her bosom. (She deftly unfastened an offending button before he chewed it off.) "Steam moves the boat under water, and steam raises the cannon when she surfaces. And then fires it—but it fires nothing so gross as a mere cannon ball, dear girl, darling girl..."

Stroking his cheek, Lady Beatrice made a softly encouraging sound. When Pickett's mouth was less obstructed by the bosom he addressed, he continued in a rising voice:

"It fires steam itself! It *projects* it, a lance of pure, shining power, Beatrice! I can slice a man in half with it! Or—" he amended at her sudden slight flinch, "—a wooden hull. And of course it can fire perfectly normal armaments as well. I am not a savage, after all. I mean to use it against enemy ships, sweetheart, not hapless sailors!"

"What enemies, sir?" Lady Beatrice whispered against his lips.

Pickett spent a moment distracted by her kisses before raising his head and declaring with shining eyes: "The French!"

$\mathcal{B}$ACK IN MR. Pickett's sitting room, Mrs. Corvey had prevailed on Mrs. Drumm for a glass of sherry; Mrs. Drumm being now in possession of the butler's keys since Mr. Pickett's outraged dismissal of that humorously inclined gentleman. Mrs. Drumm obligingly fetched the sherry, but she also fetched out a small case bottle of something else, as well as a second glass. Mrs. Corvey, unable to reveal that she was aware of this oddity, was suddenly assailed by the fear that the otherwise-splendid Mrs. Drumm was either duplicitous or a secret tippler.

"Now, Mrs. Corvey, here you are." Mrs. Drumm folded her hands in her lap, and looked at her hopefully soon-to-be employer with an anxious expression she clearly did not think Mrs. Corvey could see. "Though I should tell you, Mr. Pickett's got no great taste in sherries, and this one I wouldn't use but in a trifle filling, if you see what I mean. So if you wouldn't take it amiss, ma'am, I'd be pleased to offer you something else. Something of my own, you see."

Mrs. Corvey felt a sudden rise of hope and curiosity. "I should be delighted. And what might that be, Mrs. Drumm?"

"*Rum,*" said Mrs. Drumm forthrightly, and uncapped the case bottle. A rich heady smell rose up, somehow tropical and marine at the same time. "Good Jamaica rum, ma'am. Not that I indulge often—" and here she looked (though she did not know her auditor could see it to judge) severely at the bottle "—but this comes to me from the Indies from an old…friend, see, what runs his own eating establishment out that way."

"Why, I should be very pleased indeed," said Mrs. Corvey, who found this unexpected revelation rather charming. "I am not really all that fond of sherry myself, to tell the truth. You are a woman of broad and discerning tastes, Mrs. Drumm."

"Well, ma'am, I've seen a bit," allowed Mrs. Drumm. She poured out two generous tots and put one in Mrs. Corvey's hand. "And there's not much as startles me, at my age."

"Oh, good," said Mrs. Corvey, and took a happy sip of her rum.

IN ANY PROPER penny-dreadful, Herbertina thought in irritation, there would be convenient cover right next to an open window. In dreary reality, there was nothing but knee-high gorse closer than 200 feet to the cottages; which was where she currently lurked in the dubious shelter of two wind-bent hawthorn trees.

Rather than perch there like a phantom horseman on her peculiar steed, she elected to reconnoiter awhile. She laid down the dandy horse and sat comfortably cross-legged beneath a low branch, there to consume sandwiches and lemonade and take measure of the situation.

Certainly, there was presently no chance of approaching more closely unseen. Such was the frenetic pace displayed that men were hastening in, out and around every side of the cottages. While the lamplight did not extend very far into the surrounding meadows, the very moon whose illumination Herbertina sought to use for her own purposes would show her up immediately were she to venture out of the hawthorn's comforting shadow. But she had come prepared.

She drew her spyglass—a *very* good spyglass; its lenses had been ground by Mr. Felmouth himself—from her pocket and sought to ascertain precisely what was going on.

There were a great many bundles, barrels and bags stacked by the well, and they were being hustled down the well-shaft as fast as possible. The increase in the well-house's height was now easily seen as a portable crane, from which depended a rope ladder and with the aid of which larger bundles were lowered down the shaft.

Deduction therefore indicated that the well was the entrance to the local caves. Herbertina wondered how they bypassed the water she herself had indisputably drawn up? Watching a bag of what appeared to be black powder sent down with no apparent concern for water-proofing, she guessed that the well shaft held a removable tank, to maintain its verisimilitude for the occasional holiday-maker wandering the cliffs on a warm day. Using the pendent rope ladder, men were clambering up and down and in and out with the ease of ants on a pantry shelf.

It was impossible to identify much of the cargo being hurried down the well, at this distance and in the flickering light. Some things, however, could not be disguised. The coarse nets of coal were obvious—so, she decided, there was something down there that needed fuel: possibly Erato's postulated steam engine. There were dull metal tanks going down as well, their tops fitted with stopcocks—when one banged into the stone well coping, there was a frightened shout and curses Herbertina could hear in her bower: evidently they held some gas or fluid, under pressure and decidedly unsafe to bang about.

Interesting, all very interesting; and surely suggestive of some clandestine hooliganism afoot...

Totally damning, however, were the unmistakable cannon balls going down, netted like the coal. There was other eccentric ironmongery as well, things with linked chains and knobs and iron thorns; she rather thought Lady Beatrice could put a name to those.

All in all, not cargo for a yachting holiday. And conspicuous in its absence was any sign of provisions—unless the crew of the mystery vessel had one of those crates packed with box lunches, nothing that resembled potable drink or durable dry goods was going aboard. Perhaps that meant no long-range journey was anticipated? While Herbertina had seen the speed with which the submarine craft could move, she had no idea of its cruising range. The coal indicated they needed to refuel en route, though.

The rising moon had cleared what little haze lay on the night ocean, and its light flooded the meadows atop the cliffs. The shadow of the crane over the well was suddenly a solid wedge of black extending into the grass and gorse behind the cottages. In fact, Herbertina saw with sudden interest,

so long and dark it was that it quite obscured a straight line running between some broom bushes and the back walls of the cottages themselves. And those bushes were very near her hawthorn trees.

After a moment's calculation, she re-pocketed her spyglass, lay down on her belly, and began a serpentine crawl through the gorse to the inviting pathway of the crane's shadow. To her surprise, it was really quite easy—the gorse was at least half a foot over her head for most the way, and the drab clothes she wore became an even better Tarnhelm when randomly striped by the twiggy moonlit branches.

The broom bushes had a convenient and sweet-scented hollow round their roots, from which she could reconnoiter the area. While men were going steadily in and out of the cottages' back doors and round the walls with loads, the majority of them were safely in front. And even from her own ground-level view, the long pergola of shade was an impenetrable avenue: nothing at all could be clearly seen under the arm of the crane's shadow.

Which was quite convenient until, about twenty feet from the back walls of her goal, Herbertina ran nose-to-nose into a very surprised fox terrier.

*B*ACK IN THEIR parlor in Torquay, the other Ladies were waiting with steadily decreasing ease and good grace. The evening was running on, and there had been no message nor return from their absent members. Dora kept watch in the window seat, on the alert for any strange lights or sounds from the shore; but the town was quite silent tonight. There were not even enough pedestrians taking the evening air to provide her with anything on which to comment amusingly to the others.

They had all fallen into an anxious quiet. The Aetheric Transmitter remained silent, save for the normal low maintenance hum; which, had declared Miss Rendlesham, not only interfered with her ability to concentrate on reading *Dombey and Son* aloud, but was giving her a headache.

Maude had then declared that that was fine with her, as Miss Rendlesham's reading was not only giving *her* a headache, but—combined with the hum of the Transmitter—might very well be upon point of producing a brain seizure. Mrs. Otley had therefore diplomatically begged Miss Rendlesham to leave off and save the doubtless exciting conclusion of Mr. Dickens' work for another evening; whereupon a dissatisfied silence had fallen in the room. Jane was now sewing with less enthusiasm than doggedness and Dora was frankly asleep in the window seat, while Miss Rendlesham and Maude were sulking and glaring daggers at everyone.

It seemed impolitic to Mrs. Otley to suggest cards, and she did not care for solitaire. Sighing, she got out the dominoes and began building a labyrinth on the table, with the childish but satisfying goal of eventually collapsing the entire edifice. After a little, Miss Rendlesham relented enough to diffidently suggest that a carefully balanced card house might be erected on the rows, to provide yet more excitement with the inevitable disaster was initiated. Maude and Jane were at last drawn into the architectural gyre, and a certain amity was once more restored to the room.

They were rather gleefully engineering the fourth course of cards on an especially difficult bend of the dominoes, when a knock sounded at the parlor door. Dora sat up with a little cat-like noise, and saw all the others staring at her: hands full of cards and dominoes, all of them bent over an astonishing terraced palace on the table. They were clearly unable to answer the knock.

It sounded again. Mrs. Otley began setting her burdens down with exaggerated care, but Jane gave Dora an agonized look and implored, "Do get up and answer it, Dora! Can you not see we are not at liberty?"

So Dora got up and went to the door, straightening her blouse and tucking escaped curls back into her combs in some haste. She opened the door a hand's breath and peered out.

In the dim light of the oil lamp on the hall table stood a fretful-looking man. This was in itself peculiar, as he should not have been able to make his way to this private floor in a rooming house that catered primarily to ladies. He seemed aware of this, as he cast anxious glances up and down the hall while he stood there.

He was tall and slender and well-dressed, but bore an expression of profound distress. He was throttling his hat in his hands, and when Dora opened the door and looked out full into his face, he actually cried out and promptly dropped it on the floor. Bending at once to retrieve it, he then ran his face into the hooped curve of Dora's skirt; recoiled again with a cry, and fell over on the hall floor like a stunned insect.

Dora looked down at him doubtfully, and then back into the parlor.

"There is a man here having a seizure, I think," she said.

Miss Rendlesham came up beside her, opening the door wide. Behind them, the Aetheric Transmitter had been whisked away to the sideboard and covered with a shawl; the most outre and eye-catching object in the room was now the temple of cards and dominoes covering the table. The other Ladies stood about it in attitudes of slightly flushed surprise.

The man on the floor managed to regain his knees; then, with an almost audible creak, his feet. His mashed hat resumed its revolving in his hands like a sad dead little animal.

"Forgive my clumsiness, I pray you," he said breathlessly, "and the lateness of the hour. I am Neville Ponsonby, late of Tredway Pickett's household, and I have information of extreme importance to impart to Mrs. Corvey and her daughter, Miss Beatrice Corvey. Are they at home?"

"They are not," said Miss Rendlesham, in a voice that usually thrilled her more subservient patrons. "They are at your employer's house, as a matter of fact. I suggest you seek information there. And how did you get up here to our rooms, may I inquire?"

Mr. Ponsonby had flinched at Miss Rendlesham's stern address, but paled alarmingly as she finished. His hands clenched together, quite finishing off his hat.

"They are at Pickett's? Then please let me come within at once, I beg!" he exclaimed. "My information is become a matter of life and death!"

$\mathcal{I}$N THE BANK of herbs on the cliff top, matters had grown more serious; though not, to Lady Beatrice's mild annoyance, more silent. Although Pickett was advancing his cause with increasing determination, he continued to pontificate between frenzied kisses—indeed, it was more as though he were kissing between the points of his lecture. Lady Beatrice did not find his peculiar politics to be an enhancement to their congress, either philosophical or carnal, and in fact was feeling a certain chagrin that not even the loss of her buttons, bloomers or presumed virtue was entirely capable of *shutting him up.*

In fact, his attention was increasingly fixed on the sea below them. At length, she seized his ears in either hand and yanked his head round to face her, demanding boldly, "Kiss me, dear Mr. Pickett!" Which he did, but—as Lady Beatrice did not close her eyes during this exercise—she could not help but notice that Pickett's own gaze slid inexorably to the side as he continued his watch upon the moonlit sea.

When the kiss ended, she gave up and turned her own eyes to the view below. Thus, though their bodies contested in that most earth-bound of activities on the bed of thyme (or miner's lettuce), the lovers' gazes were not on each others' enraptured faces, but fixed in unity and expectation upon the bosom of the sea.

Lady Beatrice wondered coldly what Pickett was waiting for.

THE FOX TERRIER's hindquarters quivered uncertainly. Herbertina felt as if her own were doing the same. Slowly, carefully, she eased a hand into her trouser pocket and fetched out the last bit of biscuit from her dinner. *Thank goodness for the Devere sisters!* she thought fervently, and offered it to the interested dog.

Cold nose, warm tongue—a snuffle and the biscuit was gone, but the dog stayed quiet and was now giving Herbertina the narrow grin so typical of its breed. It was a white dog, but with a charming black domino mask from which its tongue lolled in companionable silence.

Herbertina essayed a ruffle of its forward-tilted ears and the dog huffed a little in pleasure. Now mutually reassured, Herbertina and the terrier went on: the former crawling forward while the latter trailed with nose to the ground as if it had known the plan from the beginning.

Herbertina was thus feeling some cautious satisfaction at her progress when a sudden shout shattered both the night and her composure.

"Here, ye little bitch! What d'ye think yer doing out there?"

Herbertina froze in panic. So did the terrier—then leaped over Herbertina and trotted with an embarrassed air to the back door of the cottage. A bulky shadow stood there, swinging some rod-like implement impatiently. As the dog retreated, brief tail upheld in true terrier fashion, two things occurred to Herbertina: even if she herself had been sighted, her gender would not have been apparent; and the terrier was most obviously a literal bitch. *She* was still unseen.

Nonetheless, Herbertina decided that her foray was now decisively concluded: she had important information, had narrowly avoided detection, and it was clearly time to quit the field. Accordingly, she began to inch backwards, not daring to rise or try to turn. The open cottage door remained in her full view, thus affording her a clear silhouette of the bulky shouter as he soundly kicked the fox terrier.

The dog yelped and bolted back into the meadow. Her owner swore and started after her, straight down the long aisle of shadow along which Herbertina was desperately trying to effect her escape. Within but a moment or so, it was clear that Herbertina would not avoid being seen this time; if, indeed, the fellow (still shouting imprecations at the dog) did not tread on her outright.

As the man bore down upon her, Herbertina rolled to one side and seized his passing ankle. Her weight brought him crashing to his knees; but he rolled at once, kicking out and hauling a small pistol from his breeches pocket; clearly, an experienced brawler.

Herbertina, likewise no novice, continued her own roll and came up on her feet: just in time to see the pistol extended as the fellow on the ground leaned up on one arm. He grinned maliciously, and discharged the pistol directly at Herbertina's breast.

The ball struck her like a—well, like a ball, like a cricket ball, to be precise; or one of the champagne corks more usually wielded by Nell Gwynne's rowdier patrons. It also stung like the dickens and knocked her flat on her arse. What it did not do, however, was split her breastbone, penetrate her heart, or impart any other deadly force to her person.

Herbertina was as startled as her assailant, but quicker of thought. She scrambled to her feet and leaped at him. Darting round to his side, she kicked him smartly just above his left ear, sending him at full-length on the ground with the interesting sound of a melon being flung at a garden wall. He lay utterly still.

Not pausing, Herbertina caught up the dropped rod (prosaically, it proved to be a broom) and the pistol, and strode off herself with assurance, trusting to the brevity of the encounter to lend her retreating figure a similarity to her downed opponent's. And indeed, as she sped toward the trees, a voice behind her shouted—with annoyance, but no real alarm—for "Dick" to leave off potting at the damned rabbits and get his arse back to work. Herbertina waved the broom in a universal gesture of disdainful acknowledgment, and made for cover.

By this time her little copse of hawthorn trees was also spreading a nice deep shadow to the west, and she was confident she was out of sight before the direction of her retreat was clear from the cottages. No alarms disturbed the bustle of activity behind her, but it was only a matter of time before the dog-kicking Dick either awoke or was found. Herbertina wasted no further time in observation, but discarded the broom, and ducked into the shelter of the hawthorns.

She took a moment to examine her shirtfront, in some awe. While there was a decided ache there, she felt in no way damaged. However, there was a neat hole through her waistcoat. It had evidently lodged itself against the strange new stays in her corset: *and not gone a fraction more into her chest.*

"Oh, thank you, Mr. Felmouth!" she whispered. She wheeled the dandy horse out of the bushes and prepared to speed away.

The smooth path along the cliff tops ran downhill from this vantage point, and she anticipated a swift ride down. Just before she mounted, though, she heard a soft whine, and the masked fox terrier came hesitantly out from under a bush. Herbertina paused, indecisive—then knelt and offered her hand. The bitch came forward and nosed her fingers, then sat down and grinned up at her. Herbertina patted her and rose, looking back along the cliffs one last time.

No pursuit. The crowd of men was quieter now, massing together, and it appeared a bonfire was being lit. Along the moon's road shining on the waves, a black serpentine wake was moving east.

"Well, if you can keep up, you can come with me, little lady," whispered Herbertina. She vaulted on to the dandy horse, pushing off and pumping down hard on the pedals, and coasted silently away down the path. The little fox terrier raced happily after her.

$\mathcal{P}$ICKETT LAY STILL now, head resting on Lady Beatrice's bosom. Lady Beatrice was rehearsing a rather complicated cable pattern in her head, while running her fingers through Pickett's hair in the hopes he would thus be soothed into staying silent just a little longer. Both of them still gazed out to sea where the moon struck a widening path across the waves.

Suddenly, a dark wake was visible speeding straight along that path, at right angles to the glowing lines of waves incoming. On the headland to the North which seemed to be its origin, a bonfire blazed up in the night.

Pickett lurched upright on his elbows, face alight with renewed excitement. Lady Beatrice caught her breath, startled, as other, more intimate indications were made immediately obvious to her—Pickett, fortunately, took her indrawn breath for a rekindling of passion equal to his own and set to above her with renewed vigor.

He tore his gaze from the sea long enough for a deep kiss.

"Dearest Beatrice," he panted exultantly, "do you see it? Is it not fine? Is it not inspiring?"

It was certainly inspiring him. Though Lady Beatrice took no personal pleasure from their acrobatics, she was still a refined judge of both quality and quantity—and the sight of the mysterious vessel on the ocean below was clearly a spur to Mr. Pickett's efforts. She fixed her eyes on his, widening them so the moon seemed to light her grey gaze to silver, and simply clung to his shoulders in adoring silence. He took this for the sign of swooning ecstasy he expected, and stared out in triumph once more at the sea.

To Lady Beatrice's astonishment, Pickett was suddenly so enthused at what he saw that he sat up, withdrawing from their congress with unexpected speed. He pointed and cried out in triumph.

The second mast, the cannon, had risen into the air: with a low thundering concussion, it jetted a spray that gleamed like pearls and opals in the moonlight.

Mr. Pickett followed suit.

"*Y*OU ARE MOST certainly not coming into our rooms," said Miss Rendlesham severely. Her gaze had apparently paralyzed their importunate visitor; without releasing him from the pinpoint glare, she waved one hand at Dora and ordered, "Fetch our shawls, and tell the others we will be on the smoking deck."

Dora slipped in and out the doorway with alacrity, returning wrapped in her shawl and with another to slip round Miss Rendlesham's shoulders. Miss Rendlesham took Dora's arm and pointed to the outside door.

"Outside, at once," she commanded. Mr. Ponsonby blanched and went meekly before them, wringing his hands.

Out on the deck, Miss Rendlesham seated herself on a wrought-iron bench, Dora perching solemnly beside her, and looked at Mr. Ponsonby with a frigid contempt.

"Explain yourself, sir," she said. "Why are you here at this hour? Are you about some mischief to my cousin Miss Corvey?"

"Oh, no, ma'am, I am here to be of service to you!" cried Mr. Ponsonby. "Mr. Pickett is a dangerously deranged man, and he has utterly despicable villains in his employ—"

"Yes, we know," said Miss Rendlesham. "We know it was *your* joke to teach Mr. Pickett that appalling accent, and that he understandably dismissed you for it. And now you invade our privacy to further traduce your former employer. Perhaps you are some sort of blackmailer? I wonder if we would do better to simply send for the constable."

Mr. Ponsonby appeared about to bolt for the stairs at this suggestion. Dora moved to block the way; and despite her wide-eyed kitten looks, her very posture suggested that attempting to pass her would be a serious error. Miss Rendlesham could see that her victim was ready to capitulate (although he was not enjoying his helplessness as much as her patrons usually did). She therefore sharpened her tone, and ordered him brusquely to tell her all.

Which he did not do—it being obvious very quickly that he did not know as much as they on many fronts—but what he did have to say was a useful corroboration of details. Some of it was quite enlightening. His eagerness (and fear) combined to make his tale both brief and somewhat incoherent; but Miss Rendlesham was used to that sort of response. She frowned at him severely as he finally ran down.

"Is that all, Ponsonby?" she asked, contemptuously. "You claim Mr. Pickett has engineered some underwater juggernaut, and means to attack coastal vessels? I suppose he is threatening the anchovy fleet. And he has hired manservants whom you find objectionable! And this intelligence you bring not to the police nor the harbor authorities, but to Miss Corvey? I suggest, Ponsonby, that you are a poor judge of the qualities wanted in a gentleman's servant."

"But it's all true! He is a dangerous villain!" cried the wretched Mr. Ponsonby.

"Be off with you now, you horrid little man." Miss Rendlesham rose to her feet, waving her hand in dismissal. "You shall find no blackmail opportunities here. I refrain from summoning the constable only to spare my aunt and our hostess the embarrassment of having you publicly removed; but I *shall* have you taken up for Conduct Likely to Lead to an Affray if I see you here again."

Ponsonby gaped at her. Miss Rendlesham smiled—a small, cruel, smile—and suddenly strode toward him with a stamp of her foot, like a saber fighter. Ponsonby squeaked and fled down the outside stairs, from in front of which Dora had prudently removed herself.

From the sound of his departure, he missed the last two or three steps, and thumped down into the courtyard with a small cry of pain. In only a moment, though, they could here him pattering away in terror.

"That looked like fun," said Dora as they went back indoors.

"You know, it rather was," admitted Miss Rendlesham. "So many things are tedious when performed as duty, that become a decided pleasure when one does them for one's own enjoyment."

"That's why I never do anything I don't really like," said Dora seriously.

"Well, Dora, your tastes are rather more catholic than mine, I fear," Miss Rendlesham said. "But here we are—now let us go in and tell the others, and decide what must be done next. And I think it might be a good idea to check in with Mr. Felmouth, as well."

"Do you think it is actually a matter of life and death?"

"Not to *our* Ladies," said Miss Rendlesham confidently.

"Oh, I hope Beatrice and Mrs. Corvey come home soon..."

They returned then to the parlor for a council of war.

*M*R. PICKETT WAS markedly reserved as he and Lady Beatrice walked slowly home along the cliff path. His mood had initially threatened sulkiness, but she would have none of that—a post-coitally downcast Mr. Pickett was of no use to her, whereas a triumphant one could be manipulated into spilling his heart to her. As it were.

By dint of a little clinging, a few tremulously smiling tears, and the loan of her silk handkerchief, Lady Beatrice had Mr. Pickett considerably cheered up by the time they were in sight of the lighted windows of his house. They walked slowly, his arm about her waist and her whole frame swaying against his from shoulder to knee. Whenever Mr. Pickett made sounds indicating a resumption of speech, Lady Beatrice sighed and pressed a little closer, which served to keep him admirably silent until they came to the garden gate.

He stopped their progress there.

"And so we return to the mortal world," he said, a little wistfully. "And if my passion overcame me too forcefully, dearest Beatrice, I hope you know it was the madness of a man transported for a blessed time to the company of a goddess! Will you take my marital avowal as spoken aloud?"

Lady Beatrice smiled at him serenely. "Of course, Tredway. We are adults, after all. And I accept."

Pickett's face lit with slightly stunned delight. "You will be my wife—my helpmeet—my partner in this great enterprise?"

"Have I not said so?" said Lady Beatrice (who had said nothing of the sort). "But let us not surprise Mamma with the happy news tonight, I pray you. Allow me to tell her in my own time."

Pickett raised her hands and rained kisses upon them. "I will trust to your wisdom, my grey-eyed goddess! And do assure your ma that I will go down on my knees to ask her blessing, even though you have already given me the gift of your acceptance!"

"She will be as happy as I am," Lady Beatrice told him with perfect truth.

Arm in arm, then, they made their way through the dark gardens to where the parlor doors spilled light over the grass.

Within, Mrs. Corvey was seated alone on the single divan, sipping a cup of tea and evidently listening to the sound of the sea from the open French doors on the far side of the room. Several branches of candles blazed through-out the room, giving no aid (of course) to Mrs. Corvey, but endowing the sparse furnishings with a fine flattering gild-ing. As Lady Beatrice and Mr. Pickett entered together, Mrs. Corvey's blind gaze swung in their direction. She smiled slightly, almost as if she could discern their intertwined arms from the rhythm of their gait.

Nonetheless, she called out, "Is that you, Beatrice?"

"Yes, Mamma," Lady Beatrice replied. She slipped from beneath Mr. Pickett's arm and went to sit beside Mrs. Corvey on the sofa. "Did you have a pleasant rest?"

"I did indeed, though I fear we may have stayed later than I intended," returned Mrs. Corvey. "Has the moon risen?"

"Oh, yes," said Lady Beatrice, and cast a warm glance in Mr. Pickett's direction.

Mr. Picket was pacing before the fireplace, evidently torn between wringing his hands and casting himself to his knees in front of Mrs. Corvey. His combined distress and arousal made it very difficult for his putative mother-in-law to keep a straight face, though she kept her gaze out the open windows and so off-center from his anxious figure.

Lady Beatrice gave him no opening in which to commit any faux pas, however, instead chattering smoothly and lightly as she gathered up their gloves, shawls and bonnets. Mrs. Corvey responded in kind, occasionally directing to Mr. Pickett questions to which she then gave him no time to respond; in this way, the two ladies swept him inexorably toward his own front door under the impression he himself had summoned his carriage for their use.

In very short order they were handed up to their seats (several kisses being furtively traded between Lady Beatrice and Mr. Pickett under Mrs. Corvey's blind eyes) and so driven off briskly along the drive. Mr. Pickett waved them out of sight.

They rode in silence for some time under the bright moonlight, for the moon had by now risen high and clear. As they passed that portion of the cliffs where the cottages stood, Lady Beatrice remarked aloud to Mrs. Corvey that they seemed quite brightly lit up.

"There even appeared to be a bonfire there earlier, Mamma," she said. "We could see it all clearly from the cliff path."

"The night fishing fleet, I suppose," returned Mrs. Corvey. "They say all manner of fish rise to the light of the moon."

"That is quite true, Mamma."

In a lower tone, Mrs. Corvey said, "And I hope rather more than a dozen roses results from *your* fishing, my girl."

Lady Beatrice nodded a warning at the driver before them, but smiled in discreet triumph.

"They *are* very fine roses," she said serenely. "Nonetheless, I expect they may not be unaccompanied on the morrow."

They rode on in silence then, until the driver helped them down in front of their boarding house.

*E*VEN FROM THE street, it was clear that their suite was awake. Though the downstairs parlor was lit only by a single low lamp, Mrs. Corvey and Lady Beatrice could see their own windows blazing bright above them. They climbed quietly to the third floor, where Dora popped out of their own door to wave them in as soon as they cleared the landing.

"We've had no end of excitement!" she exclaimed as they entered. "Herbertina found a way into the sea caves, and saw the gun platform in action, and fought off a dreadful thug! And she was shot at, but the new black corset stays stopped the bullet! Mr. Pickett's butler came and actually accosted us here, and Charlotte and I interrogated him and got rid of him before the landlady saw him! Mr. Felmouth says the French are launching a new warship next week!" She stopped to catch her breath and finished, "And we have a darling little dog now!"

Mrs. Corvey and Lady Beatrice stopped, staring in confusion. The Aetheric Transmitter was still out on the central table, and still surrounded by a labyrinth of stacked playing cards. Mrs. Otley had paused in sketching her peculiar skull, which was framed in Maude's lap for contrast; Miss Rendlesham had, for once, a notebook and pencil to hand instead of a novel. Everyone wore expressions of eager anticipation, save for Herbertina (who was exploring a hole in her corset with a cautious finger) and a fox terrier who was in the process of having a bow tied round its neck by Jane.

"Woof," said the terrier, and grinned ingratiatingly.

"Did Mr. Ponsonby survive being got rid of?" asked Lady Beatrice after a slight pause.

"Well, he fell down the stairs a bit, but he was on his feet when he left," said Dora.

" I think I should like to sit down now," said Mrs. Corvey. "And then we can go over this evening point by point."

They handed off their things to various of the other Ladies, Mrs. Corvey taking her customary seat at the head of the table. She removed her dark glasses and pointed at Herbertina.

"You go first, dear. It sounds as though you had the most exciting evening." Mrs. Corvey rubbed her temples. "Then Beatrice, I think—I *know* her evening was exciting."

"On the contrary, it was quite predictable," demurred Lady Beatrice, and a subdued tide of laughter ran around the table.

One by one, like schoolgirls reciting their lessons, the Ladies each recounted their adventures to the whole group. Herbertina and Lady Beatrice were definitely the Senior Girls in this exercise, with the hard information they had gathered. Herbertina's corset was passed around for examination, and the black stays declared a definite triumph; Lady Beatrice was congratulated, with some feminine hilarity, on her recent betrothal.

Mr. Pickett's personal excesses and eccentricities were reported dispassionately and received without surprise. Indeed, Lady Beatrice would not have bothered repeating them, save that she thought his reaction had a bearing on his mental state.

"Disabling the gun would likewise neutralize Mr. Pickett, I think," she said. "He has a clear emotional resonance with the performance of his gun."

"Ain't they all, though?" sighed Mrs. Corvey. "Nothing unsettles a man's feeble mind like a big gun. It's just that in his case, he can brandish the damn thing a lot further than most lads. Right across the Channel!"

This was reinforced when Lady Beatrice confirmed that Mr. Pickett was definitely targeting a French vessel in the next week. Miss Rendlesham was then able to establish corroboration with this from her post-Ponsonby communique with Mr. Felmouth—which was that the French had just launched a new warship, named *Le Cygne Impériale.*

"*The Imperial Swan?*" asked Mrs. Otley. "Is that not somewhat—*gauche*—for the new Republic?"

"Bureaucracy moves slowly," said Miss Rendlesham. "Or so Mr. Felmouth says. It was commissioned before the latest regime change. It is a sloop of war, evidently, an hermaphrodite brig nearly 200 feet long. Partly iron-clad below the water line, and the hull is made of two layers of white oak."

"So she is white and fierce and damned hard to sink," mused Mrs. Corvey. "Rather pretty conceit. Very French. And she has already launched?"

"Yes, some days ago. She is undergoing trials off the coast of France, of course, but she is due to venture into the Channel in the next three days," said Miss Rendlesham.

"When Mr. Pickett will try to sink her," Lady Beatrice said.

"We shall have our work cut out for us, I fear," said Miss Rendlesham. "Unless we just ought to disable Mr. Pickett outright, and so delay his own launch?"

Mrs. Corvey shook her head. "A nice idea, but I don't think it would stop the enterprise. It's clearly going on in his absence—he was no use to them tonight, was he?—and I suspect he doesn't run the gun crew. He's a yachtsman, a holiday sailor, not a Naval officer. I'd suspect that bugger Felan for the job... No, we cannot stop his launching the gun platform. But I think we can stop it from getting very far."

Jane suddenly cleared her throat and sang, in a fine mezzo:

> *"I'll give you gold and I'll give you fee,*
> *And my eldest daughter your bride shall be—"*

Maude and Dora joined her, in their respective soprano and alto:

> *"—If you'll sink them in the lowland, lowland, lowland,*
> *Sink them in the lowland sea!"*

Mrs. Corvey reached out and tapped the construction on the table then. With a prolonged sigh, it rippled round and down into utter destruction.

NEXT MORNING THE preparations began in earnest for stopping Mr. Pickett. As Mrs. Corvey said, while the Gentlemen might succeed in sending some well-armed and masculine help to them before Mr. Pickett's gun platform set out to sea, it were best not to rely upon it. No ship would sink because they were armed and waiting; but disaster awaited only on their being unprepared.

They had, besides, a new and potent ally to add to the mix: the redoubtable Mrs. Drumm, who was expected that very afternoon for her interview. Mrs. Corvey had already decided to offer her the position of cook at Nell Gwynne's, if Mrs. Drumm was not shocked or frightened off by the revelations of their true nature; and Mrs. Corvey felt she had received sufficient indication of a liberal and adventurous inclination to make her hopeful. At the very least, both Mrs. Corvey and Lady Beatrice were sure that Mrs. Drumm would be willing to help them stop Mr. Pickett, for whom she clearly had no good will.

Over breakfast, a discussion of the fox terrier culminated in her also being offered a position with the Ladies. Herbertina pointed out that a little sporting dog was a very good prop for a young man in her apparent social position, while the Devere sisters merely fell back on pleading for the dog's obvious heroism and charm. Mrs. Corvey admitted that the dog was, indeed, charming (especially on being offered a paw in greeting over her morning tea) but appeared to be most won over by the fact that the animal had not disgraced herself on the carpets during the night; which was, as Herbertina also pointed out, a better record than some of their patrons.

In honor of their trade and her own black mask, they named her Domina.

Immediately post-breakfast, with all parties comfortably replete with porridge and muffins, Jane tied three yards of a jolly red silk ribbon to Domina's collar, and Domina, Herbertina and the Deveres made up a party for a morning stroll. They took along Mrs. Otley's latest missive to Mr. Darwin—an envelope fat with detailed drawings of the various anatomical remains she had found—and instructions from Mrs. Corvey to locate at least two of the blacksmiths purported to be in the area and to scout the chandlers' shops as well.

"But first, a run along the beach," Herbertina assured Domina as they strolled along the street. Domina pulled so enthusiastically that Herbertina was obliged to lean well back as they made their way down the seaward-slanting street; and all four of them proceeded in high good humor, simultaneously restraining Domina from leaping ahead and Herbertina from falling over backwards.

They found the Post Office conveniently on their way and sent Mrs. Otley's package off to Mr. Charles Darwin; the distance was only about 140 miles, and they were assured he would have it within two days at the most. They also located one of the chandler shops, marking it for exploration on the way home.

Feeling very efficient, the party made their way down to the beach, where the bathing machines were parked down by the shingle rocks at water's edge. Though the strand was narrow, the sand itself was fine and smooth, and damp enough to allow a brisk walk while still remaining above the waves. Domina was so patently enthralled by the prospect that Herbertina, with a bow to the others, took her off at once for a run.

They raced the waves in and out in a long loop down the beach, and then back up again. Domina was fairly dancing as they returned, her mask split in a wide terrier grin.

"Oh, that looks so jolly! Do give me a turn, Herbert," begged Jane. When Herbertina gave her the ribbon leash, she handed off her bonnet to Dora, and the two of them took off at once in another dash along the beach.

Herbertina, hands in her pockets, strolled along following with the other two Deveres, all three of them watching the racing dog and Jane in amusement. Jane's petticoat skirts frothed about her knees as she ran—Domina somehow contrived to run at full speed with her nose to the sand, lost in momentum and some canine nasal bliss.

"There is just nothing quite so happy as a dog at the seaside," commented Herbertina. "Rather makes one wish there were something so overwhelmingly pleasant for us mere humans, eh?"

"There is chocolate," said Dora thoughtfully.

"True, true."

They walked slowly. It was a lovely morning, the sea placid as a baby's bath. A good ways down the curve of the beach, Jane and Domina were playing tag with the waves, running down to them and then fleeing with loud barking and laughter. Suddenly, though, as they whirled to flee again, the others saw Domina dart to one side, pulling the wet ribbon right through Jane's hands—Jane shrieked and sat down abruptly on the sand, her skirts blooming round her.

Herbertina went immediately to her aid while Dora and Maude made off after Domina, who was now pawing and barking at a tangle of old fishing net snagged on a bleached tree branch. Hauling Jane up and brushing sand off her skirts, Herbertina could hear the others chiding the dog as they tried to catch her trailing leash.

"I am so sorry. She was being perfectly well behaved on that ribbon, and then she just bolted!" exclaimed Jane.

"Well, she is doubtless not as well trained as we'd wish," said Herbertina. "She'll improve, now that she is in better society. Are you all right?"

"Oh, yes, just sandy. Do they have her?" Jane pointed.

Herbertina looked. While Maude had hold of Domina's leash and was tugging at it, the dog was stubbornly refusing to leave the heaped nets. And then Dora knelt down and began to pull at them as well.

"Oh!" they heard her cry. "Oh, how horrid!"

Herbertina sprinted over, Jane following more carefully. The problem was immediately obvious, now—what had suggested tree limbs tangled in the nets were, in reality, the limbs of a man. A rather dead man.

Domina danced in triumph as Herbertina and Dora pulled the nets away to reveal the slack features of none other than Mr. Ponsonby. His clothes were battered and torn, as if he had been in the rough tide a while; it was his missing right sleeve that revealed the pallid flesh which had resembled a barkless branch. His boots were also gone, unveiling long bony white feet.

Ponsonby's face was battered and torn as well, his nose visibly leaning to one side and both eyes swollen and blacked. There was no blood, due to his obvious immersion in the sea, but numerous pale cuts gaped all over his face and knuckles.

"Oh, poor man! He has been beaten and drowned!" exclaimed Maude.

"Could it not have been the waves beating him against the shore that have mauled him so?" asked Jane doubtfully.

"No. There are the marks of a ring," Herbertina, crouching down, indicated the round tattoo-like bruises on Ponsonby's face. "And see how his left eye has the worst of it, and his nose is broken to the right? He was struck repeatedly from the left side, by a right-handed man."

They all looked solemnly at one another.

"Felan, probably," said Maude. "Horrible man! Well, what do we do?"

"Cover him up and be about our errands," said Dora practically. "What else? We don't want to draw any attention to ourselves, and someone else will find him soon, when they come to use the bathing machines."

Herbertina nodded. She helped Dora up, and then began to kick the the net scraps and sand back over the unfortunate Ponsonby. "Sorry, old chap. But you won't lie out here long, I am sure."

A moment's work and they were all walking briskly back up the beach. Herbertina had Domina's leash firmly in hand again, but it was hardly necessary—she heeled sedately and trotted along with a satisfied air of duty done.

"You're a good girl after all," Herbertina told her. "You shall have a biscuit as soon as we are back in town."

*B*ACK AT THE boarding house, the daily vase of flowers had arrived from Mr. Pickett; in fact, three of them had been delivered—lilies, roses, and one vase full of flowering boughs cunningly decorated with ripe cherries and entwined with golden ribbons.

They were all delivered to the front parlor by the odious Felan, who was sporting an even more-than-usually know-ing grin. Miss Rendlesham had volunteered to go retrieve the flowers—the Ladies were taking it in turns so that no one had to put up with Felan two days running—and reported that he was also sporting scratches down one cheek and some noticeable bruises.

"Doubtless some unfortunate woman struck him," she sniffed.

Mrs. Corvey looked at the three vases side by side: the demure maiden lilies, the full-blown scarlet roses, and then the cleverly contrived cherry boughs.

"He ain't very subtle, but it's striking," she remarked.

"Yes, that is Mr. Pickett to the life," said Lady Beatrice. She examined the golden ribbons pendent from the cherries, and teased one loose. She held it up to the light, where it was revealed as a gold chain with a cherry-red ruby ring in rose gold hung on it. "My engagement ring, I believe."

"Not precisely your shade. But he must have been in quite a hurry," said Mrs. Corvey. "Still, quite nice. Try it on, dear."

Lady Beatrice obliged. Mr. Pickett's engineering training must have served him well in approximating; it fit perfectly on the appropriate finger. Once on her ivory hand, the color looked richer and darker, more like the scarlet she favored and which she had been wearing at the ball where he had met her.

With a demure flourish, she then opened the card accompanying the flood of flowers. Reading it over, she raised a brow and looked up at the others.

"I am invited to another evening picnic, in three days' time," she said. "On his yacht, this time. He says he has something important to show me."

"A sinking French warship—what a unique betrothal present!" said Miss Rendlesham wryly.

"I suspect you are correct. He says we may be out quite late," went on Lady Beatrice, "and therefore I must bring my dear Mamma along as a chaperone. He assures me you will be quite comfortable below decks, Mrs. Corvey, in his own cabin."

"Thoughtful of him, to be sure. But I think I may prefer to take the air on deck," said Mrs. Corvey. Her lenses whirred in and out thoughtfully.

"And he implores I will wear red," finished Lady Beatrice, and sighed rather wearily.

She was just finishing her combined acceptance and thank you note to Mr. Pickett when the excursion party returned at last. Their first act was to immediately exclaim over the engagement ring and flowers, though these pleasant enthusiasms were perforce curtailed by the grim news of Mr. Ponsonby's corpse discovered on the beach.

They gathered round the central table and traded the morning's news. On comparison, it had been a revealing morning everywhere, and perhaps least of all because of Mr. Pickett's love-gifts.

When Miss Rendlesham went over the injuries to Felan's face she had seen that morning, it was even more obvious that he must be responsible for the unfortunate Ponsonby's demise. Herbertina repeated her observations of ring marks on the dead man's face, and Mrs. Corvey nodded grimly.

"He's just the sort to beat a man to death," she said. "I knew we should have trouble with that one before this little adventure was over. His master's secrets may or or may not be dark enough to kill for, but a beast like Felan will kill happily enough for a lark."

"The poor fellow seemed quite fragile," said Miss Rendlesham regretfully. "Willowy, you know, and as easily frightened as a rabbit. No wonder I thought the blows to Felan's face were made by a woman!"

"Fortunately, I don't believe the late butler can be traced to us," said Lady Beatrice. "Felan cannot know you saw the body, as he was delivering flowers here at that time—and someone else will report it. And you ladies said Ponsonby was unseen that evening, coming or going?"

"As far as I know," confirmed Miss Rendlesham. "And surely it would have been mentioned to Mrs. Corvey, at least, if the staff here had seen a strange man."

"Be on your guards, girls, regardless," said Mrs. Corvey. "No one is to be alone outside our lodgings, nor speak to Felan if he can be avoided. And if he cannot be, none of you ever saw Ponsonby, is that clear? Send the bugger to dear old Mamma if he presses you."

Glances were exchanged among the Ladies—hardly clandestine, as nothing was really unseen by Mrs. Corvey; not apprehensive, either.

"We shall have to deal with him on board the *Sceptre*, though," observed Lady Beatrice.

"Well, not if I need to speak with him first. Though I can wait for the night," said Mrs. Corvey reassuringly.

"Our holiday is not turning out at all as I had hoped," said Mrs. Otley with a sigh.

"Well, we shall have a lovely sea excursion before we are done. We mailed your drawings to Mr. Darwin, too," said Herbertina. "Cheer up! We'll even have a few days afterward to catch our breath. And we did secure all the ironmongery you wanted, Mrs. C. Drills, chisels, awls and mallets. Just a pair of each, and we spread it out over four shops to disguise it—but they'll all be delivered tomorrow."

"Very good; well done, girls. Now—" (and Mrs. Corvey rubbed her eyes with genuine weariness, they all thought worriedly), "—I want the room here straightened up; and everyone is to wear her gayest gown for Mrs. Drumm this afternoon. Those flowers will brighten things up a treat, that's for certain. And I need to make sure the tea things are nice, but *not* nicer than Mrs. Drumm's own…"

Lady Beatrice rose to her feet and volunteered to go guide the landlady's kitchen staff through this delicate process. The Deveres urged Mrs. Corvey to put her feet up a while everyone else tidied, and slowly persuaded her into her own bed chamber—just like any harried respectable matron endeavoring to juggle a new son-in-law, a new cook, and a marauding murderer all on one precarious social occasion.

$\mathcal{D}$ESPITE MRS. CORVEY'S worries, the sitting room was already in an advanced state of tidiness; the Ladies themselves were a fastidious group, and the staff of the lodging house was excellent. All the Ladies quite understood Mrs. Corvey's nervousness, though—there were few things quite as nerve-wracking in a household's life as the acquisition of a new cook. And of course, in the case of Nell Gwynne's, the requirements were so much more involved on the parts of all parties involved. At least the initial security clearance was already under way despite the priority projects both in Torbay and back at the GSS headquarters. (Mr. Felmouth could be expected to have more than a vested interest in the quality of their cook, after all.)

Nonetheless, it was a matter of ordinary domestic theatre for each of them to make sure that the pastimes that showed in the sitting room were selected to impress. Mrs.

Otley made certain her sketchbook was open to an especially fine study of a living hare rather than sub-human bones; Miss Rendlesham replaced her romantic novel with a volume of Ovid (the spicier *Amores*, but it was unlikely Mrs. Drumm would know that). All sewing projects left out were of a decorative and complex design, displaying fine lace, complicated cable work and delicate stitching. Mr. Pickett's flowers were distributed about the room so that their symbolism was not so blatantly obvious.

Everyone was beautifully dressed and posed about the room when Mrs. Corvey emerged form her much-needed nap. Each of the Ladies looked supremely respectable and charming. Herbertina and the Deveres displayed a dewy youthfulness in perfect keeping with their characters. Miss Rendlesham and Mrs. Otley both looked suitably studious in their respective ways. Lady Beatrice was modestly stunning in grey silk. Even Domina, sedate in a basket by the window, wore a fresh bright bow.

The central table was set with more than enough dainties to look inviting; none of them, though, was *quite* as bright, as sumptuous or as rich in cream and jam as Mrs. Drumm's offerings had been.

"Perfect," said Mrs. Corvey.

She sat down and made sure her household account book was to hand, as well as pen and ink.

"Shall we unmask at some point? Will there be a signal?" asked Dora brightly.

"Yes. We might shock poor Mrs. Drumm a bit, but I think she can bear up," said Mrs. Corvey. "We must be in a little more haste than usual—I want her help with our projects Friday night."

A knock at the door in a few minutes proved to be Jenny, the parlor maid, announcing the expected visitor; Mrs. Corvey bade her bring the lady up, and shortly Mrs. Drumm was ushered into their sitting room.

She still wore a cook's plain black gown, though lace collar and cuffs ornamented it now. A surprisingly fashionable coal scuttle bonnet framed her face; a Spanish shawl and a flame-blue silk scarf spilled color round her shoulders. When she handed her bonnet off to Jane's polite inquiry, a lace and linen day cap could be seen sitting like a phoenix on slightly faded embers atop her red hair.

"Well, mum, here I am," she announced to Mrs. Corvey's blind gaze.

Mrs. Corvey pointed vaguely round the room, introducing each of the Ladies, who rose each with a pleasant nod of greeting as their names were called. Mrs. Drumm smiled back, though she seemed to be restraining a growing tendency to laugh. When all were named, she looked round at the various smiles directed in her direction, gazing a long moment at Herbertina. Her mouth twitched.

"Now I do see why you needed me to meet all your young ladies. A very great variety of 'em you do have, too. Which it has been my privilege to cook for before this, so it's not a shock," she said. "Though I warn you fair, I ain't cheap—it was a very *good* house, and saw much custom from gentlemen."

"So is mine. Our situation is very much as you suspect, Mrs. Drumm," said Mrs. Corvey graciously. "And then again, very different in important ways, too."

"I will just say so!" Mrs. Drumm pointed at Herbertina. "You, my lad, are a lass. Well, I say *lass,* but I doubt you're a maid-child of any sort."

"No, ma'am," replied Herbertina politely.

"Well, Mrs. Drumm, if Herbert doesn't put you off, it's my hope you'll accept my offer of employment in the very near future," said Mrs. Corvey. "But there are a few items that mark us out from the regular trade, as it were, and Herbert's the least of 'em."

As Mrs. Drumm watched with growing amazement, Mrs. Corvey took up the tea pot and poured a flawless cup of tea. She picked it up and offered it, perfectly accurately, across the table.

"Your eyes are as good as mine," said Mrs. Drumm, grinning. She reached for the cup.

"Actually, I have no eyes," Mrs. Corvey said, and removed her dark glasses. It was as well she retained the cup, too, as Mrs. Drumm's hand fell nerveless to the tabletop at the sight of her gleaming brass lenses.

Mrs. Drumm didn't faint, though her face went white as her collar and Mrs. Otley anxiously went running for the smelling salts. However, a few deep breaths and the restorative cup of tea seemed to settle her down; and though she found it obviously difficult to meet Mrs. Corvey's 'eyes,' she studied them resolutely while Mrs. Corvey gave her an abbreviated version of their origin and Maude pressed sweets upon her.

"So—they're like telescopes, then?" Mrs. Drumm took a taste of a custard tart.

"Just so."

"And they was given you by these clever Gentlemen who work for the Crown?" Mrs. Drumm gave the custard tart a look of disfavor and set it aside. "Are you—political, then?"

"More or less," said Mrs. Corvey, and proceeded to relate a brief description of the Gentlemen's Speculative Society as well. Various of the Ladies inserted occasional explanatory and encouraging comments as she went on.

She explained how the Society underwrote the cost of Nell Gwynne's, and that the various Ladies—well-bred, intelligent and educated—collected information while plying their even older trade. She touched briefly on the existence of the further technological marvels that enabled her to keep both a respectable household and a successful house of prostitution. She dwelt at considerable length on the housing benefits, the generous salary, and the appreciative audience awaiting an artiste of Mrs. Drumm's expertise. She delicately hinted at the security

assurances necessary for the staff of Nell Gwynne's, and just how many might apply to Mrs. Drumm herself.

"Though they ain't restrictive, for the domestic staff. Your predecessor departed with no trouble at all, save for leaving without notice," said Mrs. Corvey. She sighed bitterly.

"We really do need a cook. And we really are on holiday," said Dora earnestly.

"What are you doing with Mr. Pickett, then?" Mrs. Drumm looked shrewdly at Lady Beatrice. "I can't think a clever lady like you actually wants him!"

Lady Beatrice had remained silent throughout Mrs. Corvey's explanatory lecture, knitting a tiny scarlet stocking cap. She set her needles in her lap and looked seriously at Mrs. Drumm.

"To be succinct—Mr. Pickett has designed and built a steam-operated cannon. He has also designed and built a gun platform that operates underwater, and he intends to re-open war with the French in two days' time. Mr. Pickett is a boor, a petty tyrant and probably a lunatic, Mrs. Drumm," she said. "We did not seek him here, but when we discovered what he is about—and he is about some very grave mischief, as you can see—it was our duty to bring him to the attention of our masters. They cannot deal with him immediately, so we have been instructed to distract and delay him." Lady Beatrice resumed her knitting. "In two nights' time, we shall stop him. We would benefit by your assistance."

"I could poison him," said Mrs. Drumm rather eagerly.

"An understandable sentiment, I'm sure. But we think Felan is managing the crew of the *Sceptre* for Mr. Pickett, and would continue in his absence," said Lady Beatrice.

Mrs. Drumm scowled. "Felan! That one is poison himself!"

"We're prepared to handle him, never fear," Mrs. Corvey assured her. "But you see how taking Mr. Pickett out wouldn't do the job of itself. I hate to press you, Mrs. Drumm, but we are in a hurry now: how do you answer?"

Mrs. Drumm looked round their faces once more time, and then steeled herself and faced Mrs. Corvey directly.

"I say yes, mum," she said. "To your kind offer of employment, to be sure; and I hope you won't take it as a reflection on my character if I don't give notice to Mr. Pickett. But I'll be ready to take up duties on your say-so. As for helping you stop that mad bugger from starting a war—why, bless you all, I'd help you stop him from finding his next breath if that was what you wanted, he's been that bothersome! Just tell me what you need."

She and Mrs. Corvey shook hands firmly across the table, and the Devere sisters gave a little cheer.

"All right, then," said Mrs. Corvey. "Here's my plan..."

𝒯HE NEXT DAY was oddly relaxed. Only one vase of modest flowers arrived for Lady Beatrice; nor was it delivered by Felan, whom they presumed was deep in preparations for the next night's skirmish. Several tool deliveries were made to Herbertina, all tidily done up in white paper and burlap bags, and stored upstairs without undue comment. A quantity of wool grease, amounting to a gallon or so, arrived with the tools.

Last minute sewing was undertaken, attaching necessary straps to a few items and making sure all the new corset stays were in place for an evening of potential action. In a fit of whimsey, Maude embroidered a staring eye—one of the occasional sigils of the Gentlemen's Speculative Society—over the bullet hole in Herbertina's corset.

A vital question might have been—when did Mr. Pickett mean to start his marauding? The invitation to a sunset picnic on the *Sceptre* nicely gave them a time line with which to work. Checking with Mr. Felmouth verified that *Le Cygne Impériale* had been sighted paralleling the Dover coast within presumed range of the *Sceptre*, and certainly within range of the steam-powered gun platform. He also informed Mrs. Corvey that a party of Gentlemen were hoping to arrive in Torquay within a day or two; but he could make no guarantee of their timing.

A note from Mrs. Drumm, however, gave the cheering news that she had attached herself to the party by volunteering to prepare a flaming sauce for the sweet course onboard ship.

"Very enterprising of her," said Mrs. Corvey approvingly on receiving this intelligence.

"Her enthusiasm might be considered slightly daunting," said Miss Rendlesham, amused.

"You haven't come to know Pickett. Wouldn't be surprised if she planned on burning him to the waterline," returned Mrs. Corvey.

There was consternation and scandal over the finding of Mr. Ponsonby's body the prior day; the lodging house was buzzing over it. However, it was known he had lost his place with Mr. Pickett, and for a jest that—despite Mr. Pickett's eccentric and even difficult reputation locally—was regarded as quite inappropriate. His death was attributed to low living and ill-luck, and a possibly chance encounter with some transient in the fishermen's pubs.

Nonetheless, it was suggested that ladies avoid the beach for the next day or two, which meant foot traffic should be slight.

All in all, things went so quietly and so well that Mrs. Corvey declared preparations complete by tea time. A sunset walk was enjoyed by all, followed by an evening of cards and music. There was a marked excitement among the Ladies, but no one noticing it would have thought it any more than slightly giddy holidaymakers enjoying their summer by the sea.

THE LADIES SLEPT in next morning, except for Domina and Herbertina—and even there, Herbertina obligingly rose, took the terrier for a run and then came back and went back to sleep on the sofa in their parlor.

Mrs. Corvey noted it because she was up and already busy; but then, she slept little since her blindness, even with the diverting effects provided by her lenses. Some primal place in her brain stayed in the twilight, she felt, and she no longer needed sleep as much as the younger ones...besides, no matter how late she stayed up in the way of business, the hour just post-dawn was still the quietest and most peaceful time she ever had. There was a unique privacy to it, and a peculiar clarity of thought.

She had made out all their schedules for the day on separate sheets of paper by the time the Ladies wandered in, with loose hair and bare feet, like a flock of sleepy birds. It was understood to be a slow day, in anticipation of a vigorous evening.

However, there was certain amount of preparation needed before sunset; some of it was positively mundane, in that Lady Beatrice had to be dressed to be resplendent and yet be well-accoutered for action. They had brought no maids, of course, so everyone joined forces to lay out what might be needed, first for the yacht-bound parties and then for the rest of them.

"It's like getting ready for a ball!" said Dora happily, taking a damp cloth to Lady Beatrice's scarlet silk slippers. She wiped them down and set them neatly under the equally scarlet skirts of the matching gown, hanging now in the parlor to enliven its folds in the fresh air. "Except for the knives and such."

"I always carry a knife to balls," said Miss Rendlesham. She slipped one, as if by example, into the busk pocket of her corset.

"Well, of course. So do I," Dora agreed. She was now sorting tools into canvas wrappings. "But when we first came out—oh, those early parties, remember, sisters? We'd pile all our ribbons and jewels and sashes and combs together, and try everything on everyone until we each looked just right! It was so much fun. And this is, too. Do you want a mallet and chisel, or an awl, Jane?"

"Oh, let me have the chisel and mallet. I feel heroic." And Jane flexed her slender arms like a boxer, making all the others laugh.

By mid-afternoon, only Lady Beatrice and Mrs. Corvey were still in their wrappers, in anticipation of dressing for the evening. Everyone else was dressed in the simplest clothes they had brought—mostly walking skirts and good boots; no one but Herbertina had brought boys' garments or other costuming. Each of the Ladies also had a canvas sack, newly equipped with sturdy straps, wherein to transport various penetrative tools—the chisels, drills and awls Herbertina had procured—as well as a jar of wool wax. Each carried a coil of rope; a flask; a waterproof tin of lucifers. A towel.

Shortly before sunset, Mrs. Corvey looked them over and pronounced everyone as ready as they could be. She and Lady Beatrice looked iconic in the westering light: Lady Beatrice as red and white and grey-eyed as a classical goddess, and Mrs. Corvey herself as a rather more mundane shadow. The rest of the Ladies were considerably less noticeable.

"We look like romantic gypsy wenches," commented Mrs. Otley, surveying them all.

"Or tinkers' girls," said Jane, and essayed a few jig steps.

"Slip out one at a time, now, and use the stable exit," instructed Mrs. Corvey. "You do like like something from Mr. Gay's opera—and we don't want any attention. Maude, do you have your clicker?"

"I do, Mrs. C." Maude showed a cloth bag about her neck, wherein lay a clicker. Its mate lay in Mrs. Corvey's bosom.

"Herbertina?"

"Arrangements all made and ready, ma'am." Herbertina tugged her cap subserviently.

Mrs. Corvey nodded sharply, satisfied. "Luck to you, my dears. Mind yourselves, now."

One by one, each of them wished good fortune to the others as well, and went silently down the outside stairs. They scattered in all directions, so as not to make their way in an obvious group, and set out one by one for the beach.

Lady Beatrice and Mrs. Corvey waited patiently by lamplight. Domina, left behind, whined at the closed door and settled in her basket to wait.

$\mathcal{N}$O SOONER HAD Herbertina, the last to leave, vanished down the back stairs than footsteps were heard ascending from the front. Jenny the parlor-maid knocked at the door to announce the expected carriage had arrived.

It was a closed carriage tonight, rather than the open-topped barouche, and Mr. Pickett had sent it along without his own attendance. The coachman assured them, though, that he was waiting for them at the *Sceptre*'s mooring, and bowed them in.

The interior was sumptuous, and a corsage of roses lay on the back seat. Lamps on gimbals glowed on the walls, lighting the coach like a tiny ship's cabin. Mounted over the forward seat, however, Lady Beatrice and Mrs. Corvey were startled to observe a long-barreled musket and accoutrements. Lady Beatrice examined it before she sat down.

"It takes Minie balls, and is loaded," she told Mrs. Corvey, "though I cannot tell if it has been rifled."

"Must be an American custom," observed Mrs. Corvey. She patted her own reticule, where a small derringer resided, and said, "Best to keep your weapons to hand, not strewn about the place. Anyone could seize that up."

They rode on in silence a few moments before she added, thoughtfully, "Let's keep it in mind, then, eh?"

It was not a long ride; they had already learned that the *Sceptre* did not lie at anchor near Mr. Pickett's house (nor the suspicious cottages and sea-caves) but rather on the far side of the New Breakwater, in a small cove. The carriage rattled along what appeared to be new-laid gravel, and then out into a smooth path through a meadow; they descended to the level of a small shingle beach along a fresh new path filled with the scents of the sea and cut grass.

"Very rural," said Mrs. Corvey dryly. "Quite a pleasaunce he has hidden away here."

"There is a pier, though," said Lady Beatrice, peering through the window. "And I see a vessel, which must be the *Sceptre*; the mooring area is very well lit."

Indeed it was—a sturdy new pier stretched out into the protected waters of the little cove, boasting paired standing lamps. A lovely two-masted schooner was moored at the end. She swarmed with men and was evidently upon the very point of putting to sea; she seemed to quiver with impatience as moving shadows cast from the pier-side lanterns danced over her. Her bowsprit was carved as an eponymous scepter, long as a man and bound in brass: more a mace than a scepter, really, and more an unlikely visual pun than anything else.

"D'you suppose he really doesn't know what that *says?*" wondered Mrs. Corvey in amusement.

"Do many of our patrons?" asked Lady Beatrice.

"No, not really. There's none better at self-deception than little men," said Mrs. Corvey, "unless it's romantic girls.

"Lord, what a coat!" she exclaimed then, as Mr. Pickett came striding along the pier toward the carriage.

Like Juliet, he seemed to make the torches burn brighter— not by overwhelming beauty, but by the contrast of his scarlet coat with everything behind him. It was longer, brighter, redder than his previous pirate king's costume—ornamented with gold at shoulder, cuff and pocket, too, and swirling round his legs like a bloody tide.

The driver leaped down and opened the carriage door as Mr. Pickett strode down off the pier. Lady Beatrice, rather than waiting to be handed out, saw a dramatic opening— she promptly stepped down and out into the mingled shadow and lamplight, and stood there motionless with her arms outstretched in welcome.

When Mr. Picket swept her into his arms, the scarlet of their clothes mingled in a seamless match.

THE HOLIDAY HOURS spent shopping and walking through Torquay had given all the Ladies a thorough knowledge of its alleys and byways. There were a dozen well-nigh invisible ways down to the shore, and they slipped along them like so many cats. So long as they stayed off the main streets they were unlikely to be remarked, anyway. As Lady Beatrice had noted, people see what they expect to see. In sleepy, respectable Torquay—a seaside holiday destination for invalids and families—no one expected to see so many women slinking through the streets by night. Simply, no one saw them at all.

There were considerable lights and activity at the commercial wharfs, where the fishing boats and freights vessels docked. This was Herbertina's first stop, where she went up to a ship loading great bales of raw wool. It was nearly done; only a few carters still stood about, their empty carts tufted bizarrely from their loads. Herbertina went to the smallest— a single horse, its head held by an exhausted-looking boy— and handed the lad a gold coin. The boy handed Herbertina the reins. Herbertina drove away.

If anyone noticed, they would have seen one nameless boy pick up an empty cart at the end of a freight run, from another nameless boy. Odds were no one saw. And if they did, the ship was leaving on the hour for Australia. So simple.

Mrs. Corvey's plan was mostly simple—so simple, indeed, that for ordinarily-equipped women it would not have worked. They were relying on this to provide cover for them, as neither Mr. Pickett nor his private navy would reasonably expect a direct attack upon the steam gun platform. They expected to sally forth from their sea-caves, hidden by darkness and distance, and encounter their prey far out in the Channel. Perhaps close enough for the fireworks and dragon's breath of the steam cannon to be seen—Mrs. Corvey was not sure of that, but she was sure Mr. Pickett did like an audience—but certainly far enough out that *Le Cygne Impériale* was without succor.

The Ladies, however, meant to encounter the submarine gun platform fresh from its lair, if not still within it. They would disable it within sound of the surf, where neither its crew nor master would expect opposition. The Swan would sail on unknowing.

Whistling, Herbertina drove out to where the town lights dimmed and the beach was dark and silent. Just north of the base of the Breakwater, half a dozen shadows slipped from the roadside and stood waiting. Herbertina slowed the plodding horse to a halt. The shadows tossed in bundles, and began to climb into the cart.

"What a pretty boy!" said one. "Want to come with us and do something you've never done before?"

Herbertina tugged her cap brim, grinning. "Why, I'd like that, I am sure. Will I get home to mother in good time, though?"

"Oh, I doubt it very much," said Dora, clambering up on the seat.

"Sounds jolly!" said Herbertina. They drove on.

ℳR. PICKETT WAS in a high state of excitement, color blazing in his cheeks to match his scarlet coat. He had greeted Mrs. Corvey with high good humor—especially since she could not have "seen" his welcoming embrace of Lady Beatrice—and led both ladies aboard with a firm proprietary air. His hands trembled, though; they could both feel the tremor like a current in his flesh.

The *Sceptre* really was a royal pleasance, an exquisite pleasure craft. At the same time, she was obviously trim and efficient; Lady Beatrice knew little about ships (and Mrs. Corvey knew less), but it was clear to even a casual eye that the crew and fittings were superb. The crew greeted Mr. Pickett with respect and affection both, which indicated he was a competent master; they set to on departure as soon as he led his guests aboard.

The first order of business was the owner's tour, and Mr. Pickett was delighted to show off his pride and joy. He displayed the four-pound cannons at bow and stern with no comment on their utter unsuitability on a civilian craft; nor did Lady Beatrice do more than murmur appreciation of their fine crafting. As Mr. Pickett obviously assumed that she now knew all his plans and approved thoroughly, all it was necessary to do was listen to him. No questions were needed, which might have revealed how much she inexplicably *did* know. As usual, a smile and an approving murmur sufficed as conversation with Mr. Pickett.

Mrs. Corvey clung to his arm and asked occasional querulous questions as he led them round the deck. Mr. Pickett revealed an inclination to pat her arm and say, "Don't you worry, Mother!"

Lady Beatrice idly calculated the odds of his ending up gun-shot or over-sides before the evening was out.

A brief turn about the deck, though—and a grinning aside that Lady Beatrice would "soon know all!"—and he led them down to the main cabin. This, like the carriage, was a small snug jewel box, filled with lamplight. The center panel of the casement bow windows over the built-in bunk was open, letting a soft breeze in. There was a table set for three in the center, with the usual cunning arrangements to allow for maritime dining: a confining rim to the table, fixed rotating chairs, stands for bottles and carafes. But the woodwork was refined, the china, silver and napery perfect. There was already a plate of cold canapes like little gems laid out, and at the side stood Mrs. Drumm—looking serene, hands folded and her formal cuffs and collar well displayed.

"I thought you ladies might want to freshen up while I see to getting us out to sea," said Mr. Pickett. He raised Lady Beatrice's hand and kissed it. "It'll be smoother once we're well out beyond the Breakwater, much better for dining. And Mrs. Drumm here says she'll be pleased to act as maid for you."

Mrs. Drumm nodded.

Heartfelt farewells were exchanged—one would have thought Mr. Pickett were headed miles away instead of ten feet up and twenty feet over. One would also have thought he took Mrs. Drumm to be as blind as Mrs. Corvey, so ardently did he embrace Lady Beatrice before he bounded away.

"Would this whole enterprise just founder, do you suppose, if I simply shot him?" said Mrs. Corvey wearily.

"I doubt it. It appears to have momentum," replied Lady Beatrice.

Mrs. Drumm came forward to relieve both of them of their shawls. "That Felan is out there with the gun crew, too," she informed them. "He'll go on regardless tonight, unless your lasses take him. And this lot will be pacing them while Pickett romances you and capers about like a Morris dancer, I've no doubt! We're to assist if the gun platform founders, too; which it is a common problem, I'm told."

"You've been busy, Mrs. Drumm." Mrs. Corvey settled herself at the table. She picked up a spoon and checked the maker's mark.

"Well, I've offered to make all the provisions, see—not just for you ladies, though I must say it'll be a sin and a shame if you don't get to taste them—but I've packed up some treats for the crew, too," explained Mrs. Drumm. "They've been in and out of the place for the last two days, too, and hungry men always find their way to the kitchen. And they talks among themselves over the little bits of dainties I've been feeding them. Men are born gossips!"

"I have found it so, yes," Mrs. Corvey said. "Our business relies upon it, in fact."

"Nor I'm much surprised," said Mrs. Drumm. She poured out a little white wine for each of them, neatly encasing the bottle in a linen cloth as the ship's roll began to increase. "And just for your ears, madam—the crew of the *Sceptre* are going to get a real special plum duff tonight. Not enough to kill 'em, but enough to make 'em sick and groggy."

"Good heavens, Mrs. Drumm, have you poisoned everyone?"

"Not at all!" Mrs. Drumm looked offended. "I don't want us out there with a dead crew, not being able to sail a boat by myself! But the sicker they are, the less harm they can do. I couldn't see to the gun crew, though; they don't carry provisions."

"My girls will see to *them*," said Mrs. Corvey.

She drew a little shining silver case from her bodice; tiny beads studded one surface. She pressed four of these in a short rhythm; paused, then repeated it twice. A few seconds passed, and then the device emitted a soft double chirp, like a cricket.

"Ah, they are on their way," she said. She smiled at Mrs. Drumm's stare, and her lenses whirred behind her smoked glasses. "And they know we are in place. We've been busy, too, Mrs. Drumm."

$\mathcal{T}$HE LADIES IN the cart had seen the glow of the lights at the *Sceptre*'s mooring as they passed on the road above, but now they were some ways beyond it. Herbertina angled right at a descending hollow that gradually deepened to a willow-lined draw leading down to the sea. They trundled along a widening strand of brook running ahead of them to where the sound of breakers filled the darkness.

The bottom of the draw widened out to a tiny beach, where the brook lost itself amid rocks and coarse sand. Just beyond, Herbertina stopped; the others unloaded their packs and headed down to the water's edge, while Herbertina dismounted and carefully led the horse around to face back up the draw. She knotted the reins loosely and chocked the wagon with stones, where the horse could reach both the brook and some scrubby willow.

Down by the water, the others were stripping off their boots and outer clothing; Herbertina joined them, shedding her boy's clothes. All the garments were bundled into their packs. Ultimately, each of the Ladies was down to her corset, pantaloons and long, thick stockings.

"Bathing costumes would be have been warmer," complained Maude.

"But bulkier. One cannot really swim in those things," said Miss Rendlesham practically. "We will be doing rather more than splashing about in the shallows."

"How will you keep the clicker dry?" asked Dora. She began to rub wool wax over her arms, as the others were doing. "Eeeww, this sheep grease does stink!"

Maude wrinkled her nose at the jar in her hand. "I am using a French letter, and then covering it all with the stuff— it will be waterproof, then." So saying, she fitted a condom, a length of sheep intestine neatly stitched, over the clicker and greased the assemblage well with the wool wax.

"This is what the fishermen use for their hands, when the nets are rough. And to grease the tillers and such on their boats. And to waterproof canvas," observed Mrs. Otley. She made an effort to sound objective about it, but was making a very wry face as she anointed her face and throat. "Though it does have an awful smell, we will appreciate it when we are in the cold water. And we may contemplate how very useful sheep are, too."

"Sheep grease may be useful. So are French letters. I would rather contemplate the usefulness of sheep over a grilled chop and some warm wool stockings, though!" returned Dora.

"Here, Erato—I'll do the backs of your arms and legs, then you do mine."

One by one, the Ladies prepared themselves and one another. At length they were all ready—clad in corsets and stockings and slicked head to toe with wool wax. Their corsets were armored, they all had various weapons concealed about their persons, and a mood of high endeavor prevailed.

Just before they took to the waves, Maude sent the prearranged code that would inform Mrs. Corvey they were doing so. If Mrs. Corvey had any new intelligence on the location or schedule of the submarine, she would send a specific chirp; then they could exchange Morse code to elucidate the situation. If not, a second, different chirp would order them on as planned.

There were no changes.

The moon would not be up until near dawn. The waves were quiet and dark. There was a concerted gasp as the waves surged up over waist-level, but after a moment the chill was bearable; at least, so long as one kept moving. A few moments' determined swimming and they were beyond the waves, in water that surged up and down vigorously but did not break over their heads. They struck out paralleling the beach.

With the Daddyhole cliffs on the left to guide them, it was simply a matter of following the coastline. Per their plan, the Ladies kept as close inshore as they could—twice actually coming ashore at small beaches along the cliff-edge to rest, huddled together under the towels each had brought. The distance was short, but the night was chill; the starlight on the sea was very lonely.

"This would never work in winter," said Jane rather mournfully at the second stop. "Not even in Torquay!"

"And yet the fishermen assured me that the water is practically tropical this time of year," said Dora.

"They were hoping you would decide to bathe nude," said Miss Rendlesham. She laughed. "Think what we could charge for this tableaux in the way of business!"

"Bath salts, then. And hot water," said Dora firmly. "And no sheep grease."

"It does help, though. Come on, girls, we need to get round one more curve in the cliffs," said Herbertina.

"Scuttling boats ought to work up some heat, at least," muttered Dora.

Her sister Jane sang a line or two of *The Lowland Sea*, very softly, as they slipped away back into the sea like so many mermaids.

WHEN THE *SCEPTRE* seemed officially put to sea—the roll to her movement now being much more regular and deeper— one of the yacht's young men came knocking on the cabin door. In an even more honeyed drawl than Mr. Pickett's own, he invited Lady Beatrice to come above and join "the Cap'n."

Mrs. Corvey bade her *Watch her step most carefully*, and Lady Beatrice followed the American boy back up to the deck.

Mr. Pickett was at the stern with the tiller handle held easily against his broad chest. When Lady Beatrice approached, he put out his arm and pulled her in to his other side.

"I see you use a tiller, not a wheel, sir," Lady Beatrice said breathlessly.

"Can't get a proper feel for a ship unless you get your arm round her!" Pickett had to shout above the rush of wind and water, the myriad sounds of the sails and rigging. "Just like a beautiful woman, my darling Beatrice!"

Lady Beatrice put her hand on his, neatly displaying the ruby troth ring on her hand, and smiled up at him.

"Shall I be jealous, dear...Treadway?" and then dropped her eyes, as if flustered at using his Christian name.

"Never!" he bellowed tenderly. "Dearly as I hold the good old *Sceptre*, she is out here tonight for your sake—not the other way around! You shall stand in for Britannia, my Beatrice, as I strike an unparalleled blow for her imperial honor!"

And he proceeded to enlighten her in full as to their errand and intentions. To Lady Beatrice's relief, his plan was nearly precisely as they had supposed; in fact, Mrs. Corvey may have over-anticipated his cunning in setting it up. It was much more direct, more smash-and-grab than the Ladies had expected. Pickett had taken no security precautions at all—not entirely unreasonably, he expected the isolation of his sea-cave lair and the darkness of tonight to hide his activities from the residents of Torquay. But it did mean that should anyone discover him and take objection, he had left the submersible with little defense.

However, he had not overlooked the matter of publicizing his exploits. In fact, he appeared to have a better grasp of that necessity than the sanity of his plans in general. He confided to Lady Beatrice that he had written a letter to the London *Times*, detailing the entire affair and setting out his noble goals—he confessed to her that he would have mailed it already, (having no doubt as to his success) but had held it back in order to discuss it with her first.

"For I have not forgotten what a dire stroke that vile Ponsonby played against me," said Pickett. "Why, he might have cost me all! Especially you, my Beatrice...how could you ever have discerned my quality behind that ridiculous accent?"

"Dearest, I have been in no doubt as to your quality at any time. I am certain your letter needs no advice from me, but I would be honored to be allowed to see it," said Lady Beatrice, her eyes fixed on his.

She had found that a close focus on a man's eyes had a salubrious effect on his attention; in that, when she did it, his internal compass swung to her and would not be altered. Pickett had proven especially susceptible...now the red flush occasioned by mention of Ponsonby faded, and a foolish smile spread across his face.

He drew a folded paper from his coat breast and handed it to her.

In Lady Beatrice's opinion—which was considerably better informed than most young women in England, due to her past education and present occupation—Mr. Pickett's letter was actually a well-written statement of his ideals and designs. Unfortunately, it was also, she judged, practically guaranteed to start a war between England and France, should it become public—even if he failed to sink *Le Cygne Impériale*. It managed to be both belligerent and condescending, and to imply that the failure to agree with Mr. Pickett's own national ideals (whatever he thought he was at the moment) was symptomatic both of an incurable mental disease and a moral failure. Further, she judged the letter would also serve to promote a profound state of hostilities between both France and England, and Mr. Pickett's native America.

"Oh, splendid, Treadway," she murmured. "I am no judge of politics, of course, but you do seem to have hit upon every possible point of importance."

"I hoped you would like it," said Mr. Pickett, and blushed as though she were critiquing a love sonnet. Lady Beatrice concluded that Americans' passions seemed very intimately wound up in their politics.

"It is profoundly—*imperial*," she said by way of experiment, and was gratified at the way his arm tightened about her waist in passion.

In that very moment, the young man reappeared, a tray with two wine glasses in hand and a white towel about his forearm, and advised them that the meal was about to be served.

"Masden!" bellowed Pickett, and surrendered the tiller to the man who stepped promptly up.

Pickett and Lacy Beatrice toasted one another and drained their glasses; then at Pickett's instigation, tossed them over the side rather than break them on the deck. The men on deck cheered as they then withdrew.

"Does not Mr. Felan assist you?" asked Lady Beatrice as they moved carefully across the desk.

"Ha! Good fellow, but a landsman through and through," said Pickett. He swung Lady Beatrice effortlessly over the companionway's raised sill, setting her on the steep stairway-ladder there. "No, all my hands have been with me since we left the States; Mr. Felan serves in other capacities. Tonight, he's running the gun crew."

"Ah, I see."

Mr. Pickett bestowed a long kiss on Lady Beatrice at the closed cabin door.

"I will join you shortly, my love," he said. "You just go in and get comfy. No need to trouble your dear mamma with all our plans, though."

"Of course not," and Lady Beatrice cast him a last long look up through her lashes. He might have been reeling as went back down the corridor; it may have been the motion of the ship. Still, she was satisfied he was left in a continuing state of smitten lust.

Mrs. Corvey was alone in the cabin, looking out the window with her back to the door. Her dark glasses were in place when she turned to the door, but she had obviously been studying the sea outside via one of her specialty lenses.

"So far, so good," she told Lady Beatrice. "At least, we are headed the direction Mr. Felmouth said we should to catch the Frenchie. How is Captain Kidd, eh?"

Lady Beatrice actually rolled her eyes briefly as she recounted what she had most lately learned. She emphasized the letter to the *Times,* and also the lax security surrounding the gun platform.

"Essentially, he has left his treasure in a deserted place and left but one vicious dog and the isolation to guard it," she said. "Perhaps you should inform the others?"

"I shouldn't like them to let their guard down, thinking it'll be easy," said Mrs. Corvey; but she already had the clicker in hand. Her fingers flew over the bead-buttons, sending a brief cautionary comment to Maude. She repeated it, and to their combined relief a confirming chirp came back in a few moments. Maude relayed no questions, though.

"Now all we need to do is get that letter before he can send it," said Mrs. Corvey, putting the clicker back. In response, Lady Beatrice drew from her own bosom the folded paper she had removed from Pickett's coat while pressed ardently to his chest. Mrs. Corvey smiled contentedly and tucked it away inside the bodice of her gown.

"For he won't be checking *my* bosom for anything he needs," she commented with a dry laugh.

When Mr. Pickett entered boisterously, rubbing his hands together in anticipatory glee, they were both seated at the table while Lady Beatrice described the table settings to Mrs. Corvey.

Dinner began with oysters, seethed in champagne and then served cold. There were miniature vegetable terrines as well, that looked like petit fours but tasted of herbs and mushrooms. Then a clear pale green soup with marigold petals floating in it; upon asking—and being told by a beaming Mrs. Drumm that it was a broth of eels—Mr. Picket was seen to hastily lay his spoon down. However, Lady Beatrice and Mrs. Corvey thought it enchanting.

The theme of a picnic at sea was evidently addressed by Mrs. Drumm by making portions small, rich and easily eaten with the fingers. At least by Lady Beatrice and Pickett: Mrs. Corvey plied her knife and fork in a lady-like manner, while appearing utterly unaware of the play going on between the other two diners.

There were very small fish fillets in a cream sauce—easily fed in a single mouthful, easily eaten with consummate grace by Lady Beatrice. The poultry course was exclusively pigeon wings, arranged across the plate like waves in a savory sauce— it was revealed that Lady Beatrice's white teeth could crack a wing bone for its marrow with no vulgar noise whatsoever; unless one counted the muted lustful whimpers from her dining partner. When the meat course came and she proceeded to feed stamp-sized pieces of braised foie gras to Pickett, it did appear that the gentleman might choke on his own tongue; if he did not simply faint from an excess of sensual stimulation.

Lady Beatrice had read Mr. Fielding's *Tom Jones*. Mrs. Corvey began to wonder if Pickett would survive the dessert course. In fact, when it arrived—an assortment of summer berries arranged like a Roman mosaic in a mortar of almond cream—she was willing to bet their mission would end with the villain felled by a brain paroxysm. However, Mrs. Drumm deftly carved the dessert into tiles, revealing an underpinning of rich cake; poured rum over each serving and set them ablaze. This precluded Lady Beatrice from feeding Picket by hand, but her work between fork and lips was so provocative that it was a miracle Pickett did not plant his own fork in his eye.

The meal ended with tiny glasses of sherry (Mrs. Drumm had been correct; it was poor stuff), after which the participants sat quietly. Lady Beatrice exchanged compliments with Pickett, and idle talk with Mrs. Corvey for the duration of their sherry. Pickett breathed in and out, as if he had to concentrate to keep doing it.

He might have sat there all evening staring at Lady Beatrice had not she finally reminded him—with a discreet tap on his foot under the table—that he had promised to show her something special.

Pickett, eyes fairly starting from his head, pulled his watch from his waistcoat pocket and hastily checked the time.

"Indulge me just a few minutes more, ladies," he said. "I have a splendid viewing to show you, dear Beatrice, but it is dependent on when and where we are upon the sea. Let me go up and check to see how our course stands."

He departed hastily.

"Do you suppose we have been so fortunate as to have made him miss his rendezvous?" Lady Beatrice said.

"No, worse luck. Still, you all but dragged him under the table; very good work, Beatrice. The attack would go on whether or not he is on time," Mrs. Corvey said. "Though you may have impaired his judgment for a while, I fear it will not last in the face of his larger obsession."

And on the heels of her observation, a cannon blast rang out from above.

*T*HE LADIES HAD made their final swim round the last curve before the sea-caves, and come ashore. Before them lay a small deep cove, where the water surged in great slow pulses against the cliffs but only broke into a small fringe of foam on the shingle. It seemed there was no great power in the waves here. When they made their way down to the beach it was obvious why: the cove was carpeted, just below the surface, with great waving kelp fronds.

Their ultimate goal was immediately visible—a wide arch at the back of the cove, in the base of the cliff, where there was no beach between the cliff face and the breakers. At the moment, the sea almost filled it, but flickering light from within revealed the shape of the cave mouth and lit the waters directly before it.

The Ladies clustered together in the lee of a large boulder, and examined the prospect.

"Very clever, indeed," said Miss Rendlesham. "One cannot walk to this beach, nor see that light from the water, I would wager. Even night fishers would miss this."

"It poses a problem for us, though. Clearly there is a well-lit cave in the cliffs, and we would be visible even if we could get in. But I don't think we can get in through that arch, with the waters flooding it so high," said Jane.

"It is probably always flooded to some extent." Mrs. Otley was re-braiding her soaked hair, it having come nearly all the way down in their rigorous swim; she peered a little sideways as she bent her neck to reach the braid. "There appears to be a continuation of this bay itself, under the cliff. A subterranean harbor, if you will. No wonder Mr. Pickett has based his operation here!"

"So if we get through the arch, what are we likely to see, Erato?" asked Jane.

She thought. "A cave. Probably with a fairly high ceiling, as the workers would need to walk about and breathe. But the water probably fills most of it, like a tank. When they leave or enter, the gun platform doubtless does so under the water."

"When I watched it from above," said Herbertina, "there was only a wake to be seen. The gun rose afterward. I think Erato is correct, ladies; and that means we cannot come at it until it leaves the cave."

Miss Rendlesham looked out over the waters of the cove, rising and falling smoothly over the kelp. "I cannot think they go quickly when they leave. Else they would tangle themselves dreadfully. I think they probably go with caution through that web out there, where we could slip like seals. We could come at them as soon as they leave the lamplight of the cave, in fact."

This was decided, after some further examination of the area, as the best plan. It was not far at all from where they sat hidden to the entrance of the cave; one of them could have crossed the entire cove in five minutes or so, even breast-stroking through the kelp.

Accordingly, they set to keeping watch on the arch for movement. While the submarine moved swiftly in open water, it must proceed slowly when it first made its entrances into the world. The little cove had cast up a quantity of driftwood all along the shingle where they sat—it made for a good low fire behind their boulder, where they could rest and warm themselves, yet watch the long slit of lamplight from the cave without being themselves detected.

Maude sent the pre-arranged signal that let Mrs. Corvey know they were in position; no answer came for quite some time, whereby they assumed she was in company and could not respond. Before Maude was worried enough to try again, though, the confirming chirp sounded from inside her corset. Maude promptly sent a *Query* signal, but no questions were sent, nor any intelligence on Mrs. Corvey's end of the business. Whatever was happening on board the *Sceptre,* it was close enough to normal to leave Mrs. Corvey unworried.

*I*N POINT OF fact, while Mrs. Corvey *was* relatively unworried, things were not at all normal on board the *Sceptre*: unless Mr. Pickett habitually took out crews entirely composed of untested landsmen. The majority of his crew was ill at present, some of them so violently as to be incapacitated; indeed, none of them was operating at peak efficiency.

There was not a man among them that could go aloft, save at a creeping pace like a sloth clinging to a branch. Only one other man aboard, aside from Mr. Pickett, could manage the tiller without puking, so sensitive had they all become to the movement of the sea. The cannon shot that had roused the dinner party had occurred when one of the gunners setting up beside the stern guns had been overcome by vertigo, and dropped his punk into the touch-hole.

There was a definite air of hysteria on deck, unbecoming to a prize-winning racing vessel—let alone a nascent war ship. Lady Beatrice and Mrs. Corvey had come up on deck when the shouting grew louder and yet Pickett did not reappear; they now stood in the shelter of the companionway, watching as the crew and captain raced in a frenzy from one untended demand to another on the rolling vessel.

"How amazing. I wonder what she gave them?" said Lady Beatrice.

"Lightly poisoned plum duff. I must be certain she understands there's to be none of this spontaneous mischief in *my* house," said Mrs. Corvey.

"Oh, I am certain this is a response to a special provocation," said Lady Beatrice. "And it must be admitted it is useful for us."

"As long as we can get home again."

Though the crew was much diminished in effectiveness, they did manage to re-establish the *Sceptre*'s course, once Mr. Picket took over the tiller once more. The spotter in the bows, though he leaned at an acute angle clasping his belly unhappily, reported at length that he saw the expected signal light on the shore. They steered for it.

At a distance, of course, two lights close together may appear as one to the traveler on the sea. And it must be admitted, the lookout was not at his most observant; he was in acute discomfort, quite aside from having to bend over the rail and vomit at intervals. It was therefore not apparent to the advancing *Sceptre* that she was, in fact, steering for the fire lit to warm her enemies as they waited in ambush on the shore.

*I*T WAS HEARING, not sight, that first alerted the Ladies to the imminent departure of the gun platform: a hollow clanging and echo of orders called out. Thus warned, the shadow that occluded the arch was obvious—but the Ladies were already in the water and making their way as nimbly as a pack of seals on an intercept course.

The submarine apparently needed to make a straight line departure for the open sea. There was hardly room in the little cove for any maneuvering, in any event, and bearing from side to side would inevitably tangle the vessel in the kelp. This was fortunate for the approaching marauders—they could mark the approaching wake of the submarine along the line of reflected light from the cave mouth itself, and swim out at an angle to meet it. The craft itself was only a shadow in the water, invisible save where agitation broke the glittering surface of the waves into many golden mirrors.

They had hoped and intended to encounter it at the surface when the gun barrel arose, as that would have made actually securing contact with it much easier. It continued underwater as it drove through the kelp bed, though, and they would surely have lost it—slow though its initial progress was—had not Miss Rendlesham managed to dive below the surge and get a bight of rope about the vessel's stubby mast.

Warm bubbles were streaming out of it into the cold water all around her, which almost startled her off, but she had considerable practice in getting ropes around bulky moving objects. Mrs. Otley, close behind her, was equally as expert in quick knots. Between the two of them they had secured a tow line within seconds of meeting the hidden prey. All six of the Ladies seized the trailing rope, and found themselves being borne along on the surface of the sea like so many beads on a string.

There was a dreadful long moment when they were being towed along at considerable risk of being dragged underwater. It felt as though they had harnessed a kelpie and were about to be summarily drowned for their troubles. Almost at once, however, the slack on their rope increased and the gun platform rose under them. Miss Rendlesham and Mrs. Otley, being closest to the base of the rope, were actually carried into the air to lie sprawled on the hull of the thing.

Its surface was covered in canvas, wrapped all about with netting—no more than ten feet across and curving down at each side, but now that it was raised up, the top surface was much easier to cling to. The other Ladies were still trailing off beside it. They began at once to pull themselves along the tow rope, and to scrabble for the netted sides.

Just as the first of them—Dora, it was—secured a grip on the nets, though, a man's head rose from an opening hatch in front of the mast.

*O*N THE DECK of the *Sceptre*, things had calmed. Several of the crew were quite out of action, but the others were shakily attending to the sails; only the forward gun was manned, however. Mr. Pickett assured Lady Beatrice—who had joined him at the tiller—that this would be more than adequate, as they were only the backup armaments; Mrs. Corvey, of course, was not so informed, as she had disappeared from the companionway once more. Lady Beatrice assured Mr. Pickett she had returned to the quiet of the cabin.

She had not, but was instead standing near the bow, out of Mr. Pickett's line of sight and further hidden by her black gown. The crew running about the deck knew she was there, but had neither time nor orders to inform their master of the whereabouts of his putative mother-in-law; she therefore enjoyed a sort of cloak of invisibility and was able to observe the approaching action at her ease.

She was also thus the first to hear the susurration of the surf on the cliffs of Daddyhole, though she had been watching the breaking waves for some little time via her infrared lenses. She had discerned both the tiny fire on the beach and the lit cave entrance; as well as the telltale brightening of the water in the cove when the steam-powered gun platform had exited its lair.

She did not think they were especially close to shore, but she could tell they were steering for land, not open sea. She knew also that the possibility of running aground would be a powerful distraction. Accordingly, she caught at a passing deckhand's sleeve and said, "Excuse me, my lad. A blind old lady like me has very good ears, you know; are we not terribly close to the shore?"

The man stared at her—then stepped away and listened, head cocked to the side. He stared at the light in the distance. A look of horror came over his face, and he ran at once for the stern, bellowing "Cap'n! Cap'n! Lee shore, lee shore, bear away, sir! Bear away to starboard!"

$\mathcal{B}$ACK ON THE gun platform…all the Ladies froze in place. For Herbertina, Jane and Maude, it meant grappling to the tow rope and keeping their heads up; Dora went as still as a newborn dragonfly clinging to a reed with wings still too wet to fly. Miss Rendlesham and Mrs. Otley pressed themselves flat and prayed the man had no reason to look behind him. Mrs. Rendlesham got a grip on her pack by its straps, though, just in case she had to clout the fellow with it.

However, his attention was focused out to sea, where the running lights of what had to be the *Sceptre* were showing startlingly close. He gave a shout of alarm and dropped straight out of sight, slamming the hatch closed behind him.

Cries were sounding from the ship across the black water.

The mast belched out a cloud of steam, and the gun platform quivered to a halt. With no more forward momentum it wallowed in the swell, alternately assisting and impeding Dora and the others from reaching the arched top. But reach it they did, and at once stripped off and dumped out their packs. At that moment, however, the humped upper surface suddenly began to vibrate, and what was now revealed as the long barrel of a cannon started to rise up under them.

Maude was straddling it and was pushed off. She gave a cry of dismay as her chisel immediately slid off and vanished in the sea.

"Never mind!" said Herbertina sharply. "I still have mine! Get the clicker out and send to Mrs. Corvey that we have begun!"

$\mathscr{T}$HE DECK HAND ran bawling across the deck. Mr. Pickett, being a more sensible seaman than he was a politician, did not stop to question the alarm, but threw all his weight on the tiller and hauled it toward the stern. The *Sceptre* began to heel to starboard.

Lady Beatrice was thrown to port as well by this maneuver, and rolled until she fetched up against another sailor. The man went sprawling but he did stop her progress; she scrambled to her feet just in time to see him slide over the side and into the sea. This lessening the opposition by one, she did not stop to regret him but at once careened back to Mr. Pickett's side—prepared to hamper or help him as Fate dictated in completing their mission or surviving it. She therefore seized the tiller as well and pulled with all her supple strength beside him.

Mrs. Corvey did not topple, though she found herself reeling across to the rail, to which she clung desperately. As she stood there, skirts whipping round her legs, she felt and heard the clicker in her bodice chirping. There was no way to spare a hand to check it, even had she not been in full view; but as it was pressed against her collarbone, she could feel the pattern of its vibration. That coded rhythm told her that the scuttling of the gun platform was underway. Since she could also see the submarine rolling about in a cloud of warm steam only a few hundred feet away, she assumed that Maude was also aware of where *she* was, and would not require an immediate reply.

Maude was not sparing any thought to Mrs. Corvey just then, being engaged in first crawling out of the way of the rising cannon and then frantically pushing the buttons on her clicker. Having sent her message, she had grabbed up the mallet she still had, just as the hatch was once more flung open. A man stuck his head out—Maude hit him as hard as she could with the mallet—he fell down inside the submarine to a chorus of shouts from below. Maude slammed the hatch shut again, and sat on it.

The other Ladies, meanwhile, were committing various violent assaults on the submarine. At the waterline, Jane and Herbertina were chiseling a long rent in its flank; as it rolled to and fro, the gaping slit was first exposed and then submerged. Bubbles were beginning to trickle out at one end of their handiwork. Dora, Miss Rendlesham and Mrs. Otley were employing awls and drills somewhat further up the sides, but the movement of the vessel was regularly ducking these holes as well below the water.

More yells came from below, and then suddenly there was the sound of a gunshot. A foot of decking between Dora and Mrs. Otley exploded outward, weakened at the holes they had drilled, and a gout of steam and bubbles gushed forth.

As one, the Ladies dropped their tools in the sea and dove in after them. As more gunshots and shouts sounded behind them, they struck out for the *Sceptre*.

The *Sceptre* had spilled her sails when Mr. Pickett steered so precipitously to starboard; now she rolled back and forth, bereft of headway. There were only three crewmen still visible and functioning—they were scrambling aloft to the rescue of the sails. Mr. Pickett was howling orders from the stern and trying to lash the tiller down—in this he was impeded by Lady Beatrice, who chose that moment to initiate a faint across the tiller. Mr. Pickett grabbed at both, missed both, and was felled to the deck as the laden tiller swung back and struck him.

The *Sceptre* was still closer to the gun platform now. Mr. Pickett pulled himself to his feet by the rail, where he hung with the breath knocked out of him, staring dumfounded out at the wallowing wreck of his creation. Steam was belching out her side, catching faint illumination from the *Sceptre*'s lights; her stern was beginning to slip visibly below the water.

The hatch before the mast suddenly burst into the air, as by a great blow; more steam poured out. Following it were half a dozen shadowy men, who went sliding promptly off the slanting deck into the sea. Light from within the submarine shone upward, revealing the cannon proudly—and futilely—jutting erect from the deck.

Lady Beatrice rose from where she had lain gracefully below the tiller and came up beside Mr. Pickett at the rail. She placed a hand consolingly on his shoulder, just as a feeble last plume of steam escaped from the cannon to dissipate harmlessly on the night air.

The gunboat made a rude burping sound and sank by the stern under the waves.

"Oh, dear," said Lady Beatrice into the profound silence that ensued. "I am so very sorry. But do not grieve, dear Mr. Pickett—it happens to every man sooner or later."

Mr. Pickett turned a stricken face to her. She was debating whether or not to offer him an embrace (and Mrs. Corvey, watching closely, had her hand on the derringer in her reticule in case he should suddenly run mad) when various *halloos* and cries for help sounded beside the *Sceptre*.

There was no one immediately on deck to offer assistance to anyone, but the three men in the rigging came sliding down at once. Rushing to the starboard stern, they began to haul up several battered and exhausted men, all of them cursing and calling for Mr. Pickett. The last one pulled over the side was none other than Felan, still roaring imprecations even as he was dumped on the deck.

Mr. Pickett stared at them all, speechless.

"It exploded! The damned thing exploded!" howled Felan, fixing Mr. Pickett with a murderous glare.

"Exploded, my arse!" yelled one of the others. He turned to Mr. Pickett and thrust out an accusing hand at Felan. "That bugger went mad and attacked us! Stove in Bailey's skull! And then he shot a hole in the side of the boat and scuttled us!"

"I'll scuttle *you*—" snarled Felan. He yanked a pistol from his belt and shot the other man.

At least, he pulled the trigger. After its immersion in the sea, all the gun yielded was a sad little click. There was a second of stunned silence all around—then Mr. Pickett and Felan ran toward one another with mutual bellows of rage.

However, the port side stern was suddenly alive with movement as an assortment of nymphs came clambering over the railing: lithe pale figures in corsets, hair streaming over their shoulders, limbs gleaming like pearl by lamplight.

"Good evening!" said Dora, smiling round.

All the men on deck stopped dead, gaping at the apparition—except for Felan. He swerved and dove back over the rail, striking out at once with a strong pull for shore.

Everyone left on deck stood and stared at one another.

"AFTERMATHS ARE SO depressing. Even when one wins," Jane commented a short while later. She was as dry and clean as she was likely to get for a while, wrapped in a blanket and seated in the *Sceptre*'s main cabin as they put about to limp back to shore.

The wool wax had proven difficult to remove, and their wrinkled clothes had perforce been donned over its pungent remains. No one was especially happy about it, but the decanters of wine and sherry in the cabin were proving helpful restoratives.

"We'll enjoy our victory more when we are dry and warm and indoors," Maude assured her.

"And scrubbed clean of sheep grease," said Dora. "It worked well in the water, but one does not get used to the smell!"

Mrs. Corvey had had a genteel hysterical fit to get them all off deck as quickly as possible, and no great spate of questions had been forthcoming so far. Mr. Pickett was so stricken by the sudden ruin of all his plans that he had barely questioned the appearance of Lady Beatrice's "sisters," half naked and dripping wet, on his deck.

By the expedient of everyone offering explanations at once, the Ladies had for the moment vaguely convinced him that the vile Felan had kidnapped Dora for unspeakable purposes; that stalwart Herbert had trailed the villain to his sea-cave lair; from whence the others had joined forces in an effort to rescue her in a luckily stumbled-upon rowboat, which had been blown out of the water when the strange submersible craft inexplicably exploded...

The explanation made no particular sense, but Mr. Pickett did not appear to care. Mr. Pickett also did not appear willing to discuss the submarine, and in fact actually disavowed all knowledge of it when Dora prattled on with questions as to its nature. What its erstwhile crewmen thought was not known, as they had all been hustled below decks just as quickly as the Ladies had been hurried into the main cabin.

At the moment, Mr. Pickett was on deck, doing nothing. He was standing by the rail with an air of noble tragedy, staring out to sea while Lady Beatrice stood beside him. Occasionally, they spoke softly and sadly.

This intelligence was supplied by Mrs. Drumm, who alone could move un-noted between the galley, the cabin and the crew quarters. She reported that the general belief among the crew was that Felan had, indeed, somehow scuttled the submersible—evidently no ill was too great to attribute to Felan, who had been universally loathed. No one seemed to suspect the Ladies had been the attackers; or at least, no one was willing to admit it. The intention of all concerned was to say nothing to anyone and pretend nothing had ever happened...

"Mayhap he's growing some sense," she opined of Pickett.

This struck Mrs. Corvey as an excellent outcome, and she hoped the epidemic of ignorance could be encouraged to spread. She and her Ladies still had a week or so to stay in Torquay, and would very likely return again. She would not like to lose their comfortable anonymity here.

However, she was not sanguine about Mr. Pickett's ability to keep his mouth shut, nor his ambition restrained. She had also been apprised (via clicker) of a certain slightly worrying fact: the Gentlemen were waiting on shore for Treadway Pickett. They had not arrived in time to provide any help for her girls, but they were here now. She hoped it would not take too much insistence to keep the Ladies out of the remainder of this affair, which should never have become their problem in the first place...

At length, but not too long, the *Sceptre* was being warped into her private pier. Mrs. Corvey went up on deck in the cluster of the Ladies, all weary and unusually silent. They stood waiting patiently as Lady Beatrice took her leave from Mr. Pickett; they saw her put something from her hand into his. He looked then like a man who has taken a bad blow. Walking very slowly, he followed them down the pier.

The standing lamps were still burning, and the whole little mooring place was brightly lit. Mr. Pickett's fine coach was still waiting for them, its horses head-heavy in the traces; it would carry them home. But there was also a larger, darker coach standing by. There were two gentlemen waiting beside the larger coach, waiting for Mr. Pickett with an anticipatory air.

As Mrs. Corvey and the Ladies passed the gentlemen, one of them nodded politely to her; she nodded back. Mr. Pickett was coming up behind them, and she heard them stop him, courteously enough, as he made to pass them.

"Who are you?" she heard Pickett demand. "Where are you from?

"We are everywhere," said one of the Gentlemen. "We dispel illusion. May we speak to you, sir? We shall endeavor to dispel some of yours."

Then Mrs. Corvey was both out of earshot and in the lee of the coach waiting for her and hers. It fit all of them cozily—none of the Ladies minded squeezing together a bit, most of them still being chilled to the bone—and they were on point of squashing all of them into it when suddenly Lady Beatrice put a finger to her lips.

Silently, she pointed to the legs of the man on the driver's seat of their coach. His boots were wet and sandy; indeed, his breeches and coat were still dripping sea water. She looked at Mrs. Corvey, still standing outside—then she stretched up to the musket mounted on the wall of the coach, and without a sound handed it down to Mrs. Corvey.

Mrs. Corvey took off her smoked glasses; her lenses whirred, bringing her night vision into focus. She lifted the musket and took aim.

"Mr. Felan?" she called softly, in a reproachful tone. "You should not be here."

Felan turned in a flash, a horse pistol in his hand: a dry one this time, presumably. And Mrs. Corvey shot him just above his right eye. The shot carried him off the far side of the driver's seat, and he was dead when he hit the ground.

Herbertina drove them all home.

*N*EXT MORNING DAWNED late for the Ladies; it dawned about lunchtime, as a matter of fact, and no one was in any hurry to take up any activity that day. They were all so determined to have baths as long and hot as possible that they made up a party to Mr. William Pollard's establishment on the Quay, where one could not only hire a hot bath but a shower bath as well—and there was nothing better for getting salt out of one's hair than a shower bath. They came home pink and contented and dozed the rest of the day away.

Life returned to normal for a holiday by the sea.

Once, though, a messenger came with a letter for Lady Beatrice. It was from Mr. Pickett, of course, and in it he professed an undying devotion to her and to her family. He expressed his profound regrets that she did not feel she could accept his proposal of marriage, but was sure that she would someday find a gentleman noble enough to care for her as she deserved. For himself, Mr. Pickett had had a profound moment of self-realization—he was a scion of England, it was true, but he was also a son of a wild, untamed country and no fit mate for a lady like Beatrice. He was therefore removing to the new country of Australia, which was still wild, but more British than American. And if she ever heard of him again, he hoped she would think well of him.

The envelope was full of scarlet rose petals.

"What about the ring?" asked Miss Rendlesham.

"I returned it, of course," said Lady Beatrice, and that was the end of that.

And once, Mrs. Corvey said the Gentlemen's Speculative Society was still pursuing him, with an eye to somehow harnessing his mad engineering skills. But Mr. Pickett had sailed for Botany Bay in a state of high tragedy and was thus far obdurate about never returning to the Motherland.

And once, Mr. Felmouth came down from London for the afternoon, and brought them all various little toys he had devised solely for their amusement, in apology for their holiday being interrupted. He gave the dandy horse to Herbertina permanently, which was very well received.

Mrs. Drumm left Mr. Pickett's household within a day or two, and took lodgings down the hall from the Ladies.

She was able to demonstrate her skills at water ices to Mrs. Corvey's complete satisfaction. She and Mrs. Corvey spent pleasant afternoons going over future menus, and completing the security paperwork necessary for her to be hired as staff at Nell Gwynne's.

However, a few days after the debacle in the bay (as Dora called it), a couple of the Gentlemen came to see Mrs. Otley. They had with them the sketches and correspondence that she had sent to Mr. Charles Darwin. He had forwarded them to the Gentleman's Speculative Society, telling them that he himself was not in sufficient health or leisure to give these relics the attention they deserved, but that he thought experts ought to see them. And so the Society was taking them over, and they would appreciate it greatly if Mrs. Otley would turn over the bones she had so far excavated, and refrain from excavating more.

"Oh. I had hoped to name the species," she said sadly when she handed over the hat box, pink ribbon still intact.

"Ah, but it has a name," they told her. "It is called *Homo Crewkernensis*, and we are sorry to say one of our number is already investigating it. But it is a splendid find, and you will receive all proper credit when it is written up."

Mrs. Otley had to be content with that. And as her correspondence with Mr. Darwin continued and even increased after the incident, she did not consider herself badly used.

Domina got a wardrobe of matching collars and leashes, and went to London to make her fortune.

And so their oddly interrupted holiday resumed its idyll, and was judged to be, all in all, a very splendid time. When at last they left for home, though, Miss Rendlesham presented Mrs. Corvey with a great deal of literature on holiday villas in the Lake Country, as well as a volume of the works of Samuel Taylor Coleridge.

Mrs. Corvey allowed that she would seriously consider giving Torquay a miss next year. The Lake Country sounded as if it might be very peaceful, very peaceful indeed.

Refreshed and triumphant then, they went home. And August was a time of great relief and rejoicing in the vicinity of Whitehall.